THE
No. 2
GLOBAL
DETECTIVE

TOBY CLEMENTS lives in London, where he reviews
crime novels for a national newspaper, and where he keeps
a who's who in crime fiction on his desk.

Also by Toby Clements

The Asti Spumante Code: A Parody

THE
No. 2
GLOBAL DETECTIVE

A Parody

TOBY CLEMENTS

CANONGATE
Edinburgh · New York · Melbourne

First published in Great Britain in 2006 by
Canongate Books Ltd, 14 High Street,
Edinburgh EH1 1TE

1

British Library Cataloguing-in-Publication Data
A catalogue record for this book is available on
request from the British Library

1 84195 851 4 (10-digit ISBN)
978 1 84195 851 4 (13-digit ISBN)

Typeset by Palimpsest Book Production Ltd, Grangemouth, Stirlingshire
Printed and bound in Great Britain by Clays Ltd, St Ives plc

www.canongate.net

CONTENTS

Part I: A Night at College   1

1   A successful interview . . .   3
2   Settling in . . .   9
3   A tea party . . .   14
4   A welcome, of sorts . . .   25
5   But then a ghastly surprise . . .   29
6   A challenge . . .   35

Part II: The 11 O'Clock Moral Dilemma   45

CHAPTER ONE • The Tiny White Aeroplane and the   47
man in the uniform of the Botswana Postal Service
both make an appearance.

CHAPTER TWO • Mma Murakami does not answer the   53
door when Mma Ontoaste knocks on it and Mma
Ontoaste thinks this is very rude. Then, a bit later,
she has a disagreeable surprise as a new bride loses
and then, to be fair, finds, her new husband but
not without having had a fright on the way.

CHAPTER THREE • It's moral dilemma time again!   60
They cried.

CHAPTER FOUR • In which a bottle of Irn-Bru comes   66
between a man and his wife with some quite bad
consequences.

CHAPTER FIVE • Mma Ontoaste has a drunken   70
realisation but is bitten by a snake on the ankle and
then falls in the pumpkin patch (again).

CHAPTER SIX • Mma Pollosopresso saves the day but   73
    Mr JPS Spagatoni is carted off to hospital where he
    may or may not die.

CHAPTER SEVEN • Mma Ontoaste starts early and   78
    becomes a bit confused but it is all right in the end
    because it did not matter very much anyway and then
    a trip is planned!

Part III: The Hour of the Quilt   89
1   Rain   91

Part IV: Kernmantle (an Inspector Scott Rhombus novel) 127
Chapter One   129
Chapter Two   135
Chapter Three   144
Chapter Four   152
Chapter Five   159
Chapter Six   169
Chapter Seven   178

Part V: Unnatural Presumption (a Dr Faye Carpaccia 183
investigation)
1   185
2   192
3   200
4   208

Part VI: Another Gaudy Night   225
1   A conversation by the fire . . .   227
2   Landfall . . .   233
3   Unexpected guests . . .   238
4   At last; farewell . . .   246

Part I

A Night at College

1

A successful interview . . .

Tom Hurst stopped on Sjuzet Bridge to put his suitcase down.
He fumbled in his pockets for his cigarettes and his lighter and
he lit himself a Marlboro, just as he had done a thousand times
before, standing in that exact spot. It had been a while ago now,
though, and he had not been back since the trees were in full leaf
and there had been tourists in pastel shorts, noisily punting themselves along the river below him. Today the air was cold enough
that his smoke and his breath were indistinguishable, and when
he leaned over the wooden balustrade and peered at the black
water below, he could see that it was veneered with a sheet of
rough ice. He took a few more drags on his cigarette. He noticed
that his hands were shaking and his heart was racing. Tobacco or
excitement? He could not suppress a smile.

Beyond the canal the snow lay in thin patches on the mani-
cured lawns of Cuff College and the weeping willows along the
banks of the canal looked skeletal.

He had wanted to walk to the College from the station,
for old times' sake, but the sight of the taxi rank had persuaded
him otherwise. The driver took him the long way round and
Tom said nothing until they were passing the war memorial
on Launcester Street, five minutes from the College gates,

when he asked to be dropped off. The driver hadn't been surprised.

'Cuff College is it, mate?' he asked in the mirror. Tom nodded. 'Going back then are you? It's what they all want. They all want to be dropped here so they can walk the last few yards themselves. Something about that place.'

The driver gestured down Musgrave Street,[1] crowded with overhanging medieval houses, towards the College. Tom paid his fare and the driver pulled away with an ironic salute, leaving him standing there for a moment under the shadow of the languishing soldier, dusted today with snow crystals and verdigris. He read the inscription again, although he knew it by heart:

> As through the field he walked alone,
> By chance he met grim Death,
> Who with his dart did strike his heart,
> And rob him of his breath.

Doggerel, of course, but nonetheless.

Tom shivered suddenly, the cold penetrating his coat, and he set off briskly up the deserted street. Not much had changed since he had been a student. The tailor was still there, closed today, as was the solicitors' office, but a branch of an American coffee chain had ousted The Olde Tea Shoppe. Thank God for that, he thought. He could remember the taste of the Tea Shoppe's over-brewed tea as if he had drunk it only yesterday, and the stale buns and the condensation that fogged the window and dripped from the ceiling. How many hours had he spent in there, he wondered. He could

---

1 For the purposes of this book I have put Seaton Street as running parallel between Pilton Place and Andover Street, behind Colchester College.

recall Margaret – probably not her real name, but at the time, who cared – the woman who waited on tables, always with that plaster on her thumb, invariably dipped in whatever you were about to eat or drink. She was Scotch, almost needless to say.

It was strange how memories of life at Oxford seemed universal. Everybody had them. One had only to mention a word such as 'scout' or 'parkin' or 'Encænia' and mouths would start to water in reminiscence. Tom could recall scaling Magdalen tower before dawn one May Day and feeling it sway as the bells began to peal. The strange thing was that he knew he had never done any such thing.

Cuff College: alma mater of all the great literary sleuths, as well as most of their sidekicks and, occasionally – and this was the equivalent of getting a third – the friends of the genius detective with whom the ordinary reader could identify. Sometimes the villains too, of course. It was a neo-Gothic building of honey-coloured stone, handsome and not too pretentious, built in land-scaped grounds hard by the river. A central quadrangle was surrounded by rooms for the undergraduates and Fellows, but it was the library that made it the institution it was. The library held every crime-fiction book ever published in any language and was a Mecca for plagiarists. The College ran courses in the summer for authors seeking refresher courses, or those from other genres who wished to experiment without committing to crime fiction forever.

As Tom stood on the bridge – named after the term for the narration of a detective story – he found himself recalling his first visit to Cuff College, when he had been an undergraduate hoping to follow his father, and his father's father, in the Genre. He had been welcomed that time by the Admissions Tutor: a balding man with a handsome pair of moustaches and a strong but not immediately placeable European accent. The man had asked a few questions about Tom's father, of course, and his father's father, just as Tom had hoped he might not: his father had been one of the stars of the Genre, exciting great expectations, until he had jumped genre and taken up writing Romantic novels under the name of Violet O'Shaughnessy. Nothing had been the same since.

Still, after a pause the Admissions Tutor had stood up and offered Tom his hand and a place in the class of '97.

Tom's most recent interview had taken place just a few weeks earlier, after an envelope made of dense cream card had landed on his parents' mat, the handwriting immediately urgent. It was a summons to an old-fashioned club off Pall Mall in London. The Dean would be in town for a day and might Tom be interested to meet him to discuss a post at Cuff College? He had replied in the affirmative, hardly able to believe it, and three days later he met the Dean – a tall, slim man with the extravagant eyebrows of an emperor penguin and an emerald-green smoking jacket with frogging on the lapels – in the Morning Room, by the fire, under a portrait of Wilkie Collins. The room was all leather chairs, thick carpet, table lamps and mahogany panelling. A sherry and a mince pie each.

'Such a great man,' the Dean had trilled, a long-fingered hand gesturing to the portrait above them. Tom had nodded, his mouth dry, small talk not being his stock in trade. A silence had followed. The fire was uncomfortably warm on his legs and he thought he could smell damp wool beginning to singe.

'You are right,' said the Dean, after an awkward second. He drew a hand through his thick grey thatch and Tom noticed – as he had studied to – a vein flickering in the older man's temple: a sign of strain, perhaps? Or the early indications of a future embolism? The Dean's pale gaze flicked around the room before settling back on Tom. He smiled unconvincingly.

'Yes,' he said. 'Now, where were we, hmmm? Ah! Yes. The fact of the matter is – the fact of the matter is that we are—'

And here, hardly started, he gave a shiver and bit his lip.

'—we are anticipating a vacancy.'

The vacancy turned out to be Junior Tutor in Transgression and Pathology – Tran and Path. Tom could hardly believe it. Such vacancies were rare and, as a rule of thumb, filled internally by someone with some experience in the genre. This was a chance that he could hardly have dared wait for. To Tom, mired in depression after Serena's death, and the trial that had followed, it was the chance to start again.

'Your students are the usual mixed bunch. One or two with genuine promise. Others – well, you'll see.'

They agreed terms and three months' probation. Two lectures a week, five undergraduates to supervise to start with and a paper to write by the end of the academic year if he wanted to renew his tenure. But the Dean was distracted and hardly seemed to care one way or the other. Two things immediately puzzled Tom: the first was the vacancy.

'An illness,' explained the Dean, in careful cadence, holding Tom's eye as if to dare him to ask another question. 'We thought it would be temporary, over in a few months, you understand, but these things run on. You know how it is.'

Tom had wondered at the phrase 'these things' but was anxious to get on to the other question: why him? There were thousands more able and better qualified than he.

'A recommendation, my boy,' replied the Dean, finding once again the ability to twinkle.

From whom?

'Our librarian.'

Tom squinted.

'A Miss Appleton,' the Dean declaimed, letting the words echo grandly around the room. 'A Miss Alice Appleton.'

'Alice Appleton?' Tom blurted. '*Alice* is working in your library?'

The Dean nodded, a smile playing around his lips. Alice Appleton. For a second Tom was winded by the sound of her name, and there was a sharp heat in his chest. Alice Appleton. He had not heard it spoken aloud for more than a year now, but it had never been far from his mind.

Alice Appleton.

He took one last pull on his cigarette before carefully grinding it out on the rail. He flicked the stub into the river and watched it melt through the ice with a hiss.

2

Settling in . . .

'And this is your room,' Matron said with a lopsided smile, opening the door to a space no bigger than a prison cell. There was just enough room for a single bed, a scarred desk, a sink and – and he was glad to see this – a waste-paper basket. He remembered his own supervisor when he had been an undergraduate telling him that the waste-paper basket would always be his best friend. How right he had been, thought Tom, picturing all those bins full of telltale balls of screwed-up foolscap that had followed him wherever he went, and were all he had to show for himself so far.

In one corner there was a stone fireplace that seemed to be funnelling cold air into the room and above it hung a portrait of some Tudor grandee's wife in dark oils who reminded Tom of Margaret from the Tea Shoppe. They were on the fourth floor with a view across the Old Quad and through the ill-fitting casement window he could see that a new flurry of snow looked like settling on the roofs opposite.

'It isn't much, I know,' Matron said behind him. He was aware of her gaze fixed on him. For want of some distraction, he turned on one of the taps with a squeak to let loose a dry sprinkling of rust flakes.

'Oh dear,' she said 'No one has used this room since . . .'

She stopped herself.

'Well, for a long time.'

She was elderly, with a rheumy eye, her accent faintly ginny and pre-war. He remembered her as a younger woman when he had been an undergraduate, but doubted she would have recalled him unless reminded. He put his suitcase on the unyielding bed and sought to reassure her.

'Oh, it's fine, Matron, honestly. I couldn't have asked for anything better. I'll be right in the thick of things here.'

His breath bloomed in the icy air. Matron nodded quickly and glanced at the watch hanging upside down on her bosom with a practised tuck of the chin.

'The Dean will meet you in his room in about ten minutes,' she said. 'Give you time to—'

Her eye strayed to the tap.

'—*wash* and so forth. The bathroom is along the corridor. No baths to be taken after eleven in the evening or before seven in the morning, and if you wouldn't mind taking care not to use too much hot water, I'm sure the other Fellows would appreciate it.'

Tom smiled and thanked her and she was just about to leave when she ducked back into his room.

'Mr Hurst,' she whispered urgently, her eyes fixing his in some grip he could only struggle to resist.

'Can I just say how pleased we all are that you have come to help? It hasn't been easy here these past months, as you can imagine, but with you here – well, I think we'll all rest a great deal more easily.'

Tom nodded, the sort of nod you give to get rid of an elderly drunk in the street, and he stood with a glassy smile on his face as she closed the door behind her. What on earth could she have meant? What hadn't been easy? Tom began unpacking his suitcase and found himself standing, stalled, with a pile of shirts in his hand looking for somewhere to put them. His room had no furniture. Perhaps there was a chest of drawers in the corridor?

He opened the door and was about to step out when he felt, or rather sensed, a movement in the gloom. His skin froze in prickles. He was instantly sure the movement was not random, but a reaction to his arrival. This is good, he thought, with a slight thrill of recognition, remembering his lessons. Basic Solipsistic Paranoia – a prerequisite of the top-flight sleuth.

'Hello?' he called.

No reply. And yet he was sure he had not imagined the movement. There was something about the quality of the silence, as if it were holding its breath. He retreated into his room, put the shirts back in his suitcase and then tiptoed softly along the corridor, keeping to the outside edges where he imagined the boards would creak less. Around him the light was dim and diffuse. The walls were punctuated by doors that seemed long locked. On each was a label, encased in a dull brass holder, indicating the name of the occupant in spidery copperplate: Cordelia Gray; Arsène Lupin; Srnt. Maj. Samuel B Steele; Susan Silverman.

'Hello?' he tried again, approaching the end of the corridor. There was a furtive scurrying movement, the suggestion of a slight sibilance, the click of the latch of a door and then the sound of well-shod feet running quickly down spiralling stone stairs.

'Wait!' shouted Tom, turning the corner of the corridor. There was a door to some stairs. He jerked it open.

'Come back!' he shouted down the stairs after the footsteps. He was answered only by a strange shrill laugh and a sudden harsh gust of warm air that blasted him in the face until it was cut off with the bang of a heavy door. Tom ran to the window and tried to peer down into the Quad; nothing. He was about to turn again and run down the stairs when he saw, from the corner of one eye, the handle of one of the doors – room number one hundred and thirteen – turn slowly from within. He stepped back to wait. The door remained shut.

'Who's that?' demanded Tom.

The handle stopped turning.

'Who are you?' he asked again, examining the label in the brass clip. It was blank. Tom knocked on the door. The door remained shut. He knocked again.

'Hello? Anyone in there?'

Tom stood back and then crouched to look under the door. He could see the soles of two stout black shoes and what he took to be the rubber tip of a walking stick. Whoever it was stayed absolutely still. A warm draught flooded from the cracks around the door. Tom straightened up and knocked again.

He tried to speak but his throat was dry. He felt suddenly vulnerable and when he did manage to force out some words his voice fluctuated and caught unpredictably.

'Hello, in there. Sorry for disturbing you. I thought I heard something – someone, I should say – in the corridor.'

There was no reply. Tom put his ear to the panel. There was a wheezed inhalation and then nothing. Complete silence. He listened again. Nothing. Only perhaps a faint smell. What though? Something familiar yet also – no, he could not place it. He listened again. Then he heard it. A rasping, whispery voice.

'Go away. Go away now. Get away from here before it is too late.'

Tom stepped back again. He stared at the door, his eyes wide and round, the hair on his neck on end.

After a second he shook his head and returned to his room. He was being stupid, he reasoned. He noticed the label on his own door read just 'Wormwood'. What did he expect, he wondered? This was Cuff College. Of course there would be running feet, locked doors, unexplained disappearances and strange smells.

He was smiling to himself until he turned and saw something that made him shrink back in terror. Hanging from a nail driven into the wall, a small crudely carved wooden doll with a long hatpin sticking from a bloody wound in her chest. Under her someone had carved some words that made Tom step back in terror: The Dean and Prof. Wikipedia are bum chums.

'Bum chums?' he said aloud. Did people say such things anymore?

3

A tea party . . .

'Ah, Hurst, my dear boy, there you are at long last. Settled in all right, eh? That's the job.'

Once again the Dean was standing by a fire, under another portrait of Wilkie Collins, with what looked like a *pastis* in his hand. The only differences from the first time they had met were that he had shed his smoking jacket and there were, post-Christmas, no mince pies. Instead he was wearing a white shirt, pristine, gathered with articulated steel bands just above the elbows, and some skull-and-crossbones cufflinks. A present from an indulgent nephew, perhaps. He looked well, slightly tanned perhaps, and the vein that Tom had noticed before Christmas no longer throbbed in the Dean's temple.

The Dean waved Tom to one of the two leather chesterfields and retreated behind his own magnificent dark wood partner's desk. The fire spat and the ice in the Dean's glass chinked[2] as he put it down on the leather blotter. Tom sat. It was ostentatiously civilised.

2 Readers should note the inversion of the moral universe here, so that where cold would ordinarily represent bad, and warm good, here they represent their opposites. I do not suppose this is the last time I will muddle something up.

'Good Christmas? New Year?' the Dean asked, careless of the answer, shuffling through his papers looking for something.

Tom thought for a moment. He recalled a few long days with his parents: his mother absenting herself in the kitchen, his father sitting in the armchair in front of the fire, deep in a Danielle Steele novel.

'Quiet,' he said.

'Hmmm,' approved the Dean absently. 'I always like to get some sun, myself.'

The Dean's room seemed designed to give away nothing more than the obvious: that he was a bookish dandy who kept his whisky in a heavy cut-glass decanter; his taste in art was orthodox to the point of nullity and he liked to keep his room warm. There was a series of framed photographs – portraits – on the wall. Past Deans of the College, by the look of them, in their fur-lined academic gowns. They were names Tom would know, of course. Some of the most famous names in the Genre. From where he was sitting he could see a photograph of a man with a very large head – he must, thought Tom, wear a size-eight hat.

The Dean now had a sheaf of papers for Tom to sign and a 'chit' that he explained was redeemable from a tailor in town for one of the long black gowns similar to his own, although without the silk-lined hood. Together they went through the timetable for Tom's lectures – two a week – and the list of his undergraduates. They were, as the Dean had suggested, a mixed bunch.

'I understood I was to supervise just five students,' Tom said. 'Yet I see six names here? I am not complaining, you understand, but perhaps it is a mistake? One name is repeated. Chowdhury? Or are they siblings?'

'Ah yes,' agreed the Dean. 'Chowdhury. Rather awkward. Chowdhury is – are? – Siamese twins. Joined at the head. Twice the brains; double the insight. I'm expecting great things of them. There aren't many in the Genre from the subcontinent. Can't think why.'

It seemed that Tom was also to supervise an Argentinian gaucho, a Chinese tumbler and a man skilled at deep-sea diving. There was also a woman bus driver. The Dean tutted when he read out her name.

'Means she can only solve crimes committed on bus routes.'

Tom was pleased to see that the fashion for Scandinavian detectives seemed to have waned in favour of the more exotic.

'This one's a Tuareg.' The Dean pointed at an unfamiliar name. 'Knows a lot about camels and the desert and so forth. According to his CV he can track week-old footprints across dry sand, but he doesn't talk much. Worried sand will get in his mouth, I suppose. And with that headgear on, you can't see much of his face. Not a pull for the film rights, is it? Still, he is supposed to be very loyal and he might make a decent sidekick in something light. I won't say you haven't got your work cut out there, though.'

The Dean glanced at his watch.

'Now I hope you don't mind, Tom, but I've asked some of the members of staff to join us for tea. Your first chance to meet them, although no doubt you'll know some of them by their work. And you ought to meet Claire.'

'Claire?'

'Claire Morgan. Your head of department.'

The Dean took on a slightly uncomfortable look as he said her name. Distant alarm bells began ringing in Tom's mind again. Why had a vacancy come up mid-year? What *had* happened to his predecessor? Why had he not met his head of department before he was given the post? Something was wrong, but what?

He was about to ask when the Dean continued.

'I ought to warn you, though, that Claire can be rather—' he paused, searching for the right word. He found it: 'Abrupt. Particularly if she has had a drop to—'

There was a heavy knock at the door and it opened before the Dean had time to say anything else. It was a heavy-set, formidable-looking woman in her middle age, wearing a teal-blue three-piece tweed trouser suit and a gold-rimmed monocle. Her greying hair was drawn back, but wildly, and her craggy face was ruddy. As the door opened Tom saw she was consulting a large, handsome half-hunter watch, which, once she had announced the time – four o'clock exactly – in a contralto voice, she pocketed in her waistcoat, leaving a heavy chain stretching across her substantial girth.

'DEAN!' she boomed, making the Dean flinch.

'Hello, Claire, I am glad you're here first—'

'Always punctual, Dean. You said four o'clock. It is four o'clock and so HERE I AM!'

'Yes,' mumbled the Dean. 'Good stuff. Now, Claire, this is Tom Hurst, your new Junior Lecturer.'

Claire turned to squint at Tom through her monocle. He felt as if he were something on a plate that the Dean was offering in the same manner as a waiter trying a new dish on a tricky but important diner. He knew he might be sent back at any moment.

'So this is HE!' she bellowed, loud enough to make the ice in the Dean's whisky shift. 'The Dean has TOLD me about you.'

Flecks of sputum flew from a mouth in which her teeth were square and yellow, like those Spanish snacks the name of which Tom could not instantly recall. Anyone could have smelled the drink on her from a hundred paces. Tom forced a smile and proffered his hand. She recoiled.

17

'NEVER shake hands! Can't bear to TOUCH people! Hate to think where that hand's BEEN, you see! KNOW too much about 'em, I do!'

Tom shrugged as if he sympathised, but then could suddenly think of nothing to do with his hands. He clasped them with a slight clap.

'Stand still, will you!' she snapped. 'Let me have a look at you! Hmmm. Good seat. Like your father's and I dare say you father's father before him. Runs in the family, you know, Dean, FROM THE PATERNAL SIDE.'

The Dean raised his eyebrows.

'Really?'

'You DON'T believe me.'

She said this as if she were somehow disappointed, as if the Dean had just let her down, but before she could take it any further there was a sharp rap on the door.

'Come!' cried the Dean, clearly relieved. Claire harrumphed and took a step back, subsiding with a rumbling sigh into one of the chesterfields, her back to the door just as it opened. In came a willow wand of a man clutching a small pile of leather-bound books.

'Dean—' the man began in a high querulous voice, ignoring Tom and walking into the Dean's study with quick dainty steps. 'Dean, I weally must pwotest at this term's we-allocation of pigeon holes—'

The Dean was in no mood to hear his protestations.

'Yardley,' he said. 'This is hardly the time. I've asked you here to meet our newest member of staff: Tom Hurst. Tom is joining us to help out with Tran and Path, aren't you, Tom? And you know Claire, of course. Tom, this is Professor Yardley, Lecturer in Formalist Fiction and Socio-Political Critique.'

Yardley – wearing a well-cut brown suit, a yellow waistcoat and, almost inevitably, to Tom's eyes, a mulberry bow-tie – stopped mid-stride and, with hardly a glance at Tom, he pulled a sickly and wholly unconvincing smile of joy at seeing Claire.

'Claire—' he began, his voice thick with treacle.

'It won't work, you know, Yardley!' Claire barked. 'I'll not lecture from RUBBISH.'

'Wubbish?' said Yardley. 'I hardly know what you're talking about, Claire.'

'Your book. The one that should never have been published. I know you want me to set it as a course text but I won't, you know, because it's *wubbish*. It's bunkum. You UNDERSTAND me, man?'

Yardley gaped a couple of times, struggling for breath, before withdrawing a folded square of canary-yellow linen from his breast pocket and dabbing at his bulbous brow. Before he was required to come back with a face-saving answer, there was a soft knock on the door and in came a battered trolley on which some tea things tinkled gently on its top shelf. Behind it shuffled an elderly woman in a housecoat.

'Here we are,' she said, more to herself than anyone else. Her voice was grandmotherly and Tom was sure he could smell roses.

'Oh not those BLOODY old fairy cakes again!' barked Claire from her position on the chesterfield. The tea lady – her face the shape of a scone, including dabs of flour on one cheek – looked up in surprise. Her periwinkle-blue eyes began to water.

'But I made them myself,' she stammered.

'I thought you might've,' Claire said. 'They're horrible. Disgusting. Why don't YOU BUY SOME IN?'

'Claire,' began the Dean. 'Steady on. Please.'

'I tell it like it is, Dean, you should know that by now. Her cakes – I don't like to call them fairy cakes, in the company of Yardley here – are dis-GUSTIN''

'Well, Mrs Robinson, I will certainly have one of your cakes. I think they are delicious.'

The Dean helped himself as Mrs Robinson poured the tea. She was snivelling slightly, and a drop of something clung to the end of her nose, threatening to fall into someone's teacup. Yardley came and stood beside Tom.

'She can be wather abwasive,' he said, referring, Tom guessed, to Claire.

'Yes,' agreed Tom. 'So I see.'

'I wonder if you have read my latest work? The Pwototype and its Successive Wepwoductions: Magnum P.I., Higgins and the Poly-Industwial in Cwime Fiction Today?'

Tom shook his head.

'Pity,' said Yardley, drifting away.

Once again there was a knock at the door.

'Only us!' cried a bright-voiced girl as she popped her head around the door, a ponytail of gathered blonde hair swinging gaily around her chin. She was flushed from the cold or exercise and someone seemed to be playfully pushing her in from behind. Tom saw she was wearing old-fashioned tennis clothes. Behind her came a young man with a receding hairline, also in vintage tennis gear, including a cable-knit sleeveless sweater. He was carrying a couple of Dunlop max-ply rackets and a tube of balls. His arms were thin and very hairy and the skin seemed almost green.

'We've just had the first set of the year!' he exclaimed in a deep voice. 'So invigorating! You should all try it, you know!'

'Ah! The two lovebirds,' smirked the Dean, hoping for some respite from Claire. 'How was it?'

'Wonderful! Although Rex will keep hitting those cross-court dinks!'

Introductions were made. Celia and Rex were Junior Research Fellows. He was writing his paper on the function of the personal trainer in Crime Fiction, hers was to be on the role of the mannequin. They were engaged to be married in the summer. Rex had a powerful grip.

'Good to meet you,' he confirmed, crushing Tom's fingers. His breath was sour and Tom could not help but flinch. Celia made a fuss of Mrs Robinson and her tea cakes and it looked as if things were calming down again when Claire Morgan spoke up.

'No one's FOOLED, you know?' she said.

This was aimed at Rex. The room froze.

'Sorry?' Rex said, his face tensing.

'I said no one's fooled. You act like a twenty-year-old but we can all see you're nearer fifty. What did ye think of the handshake, Tom? Nearly broke your bones, I'll warrant. He's very proud of that, is Rex. Thinks it makes him appear virile. Manly. We all know what it is, don't we? An ONANIST'S HANDSHAKE.'

'Claire!' snapped the Dean.

'He's got the grip of a compulsive masturbator. Look at yourself, man! Your head is like a skull! Love's young dream? BUMS AND FISHCAKES, more like!'

'Claire!' spluttered Celia. 'You can't talk to my fiancé like that!'

'Oh BE QUIET. I've had enough of you. What? Three engagements is it now? Three rings, eh? No doubt your WEDDING DRESS IS WHITE!'

Celia burst into tears. Rex looked rattled – Claire's revelation was obviously news to him – and was almost unable to take Celia by the shoulders and lead her away.

Just then there was another knock at the door. The Dean shifted uncomfortably. Two more people appeared: an old lady with a cloud of white hair under a hat that looked more like a tea cosy, and a tall thin man in a slightly shabby but beautifully cut racing suit.

'Ah,' muttered the Dean again, but half-heartedly this time. Things were obviously not going to plan and he was no longer enjoying himself.

'Miss Featherstonehaugh! Lord Denbeigh! So glad you could make it. Do come in and help yourself to tea. You will not have met Tom Hurst. Our new Junior Lecturer in Tran and Path.'

Denbeigh, whippet-thin and with a sheaf of blond hair swept back over one permanently cocked eyebrow, shook Tom's hand, mumbling a stream of only vaguely intelligible patrician vowels, while Miss Featherstonehaugh blinked at him kindly and mewed something about the weather. Denbeigh guided Miss Featherstonehaugh to the chesterfield opposite Claire. He helped her settle herself with her appliqué bag of knitting.

'There you are m'dear,' he drawled, hardly opening his mouth to speak. 'I'll fetch you a cup of tea?'

The old lady nodded gratefully and fussed with her knitting for a second before, suddenly aware that she was being watched, she looked up. Claire was glaring across at her.

'Well, if it isn't old Miss Marple herself,' she started. 'Knit, knit, KNIT, you old NITWIT.'

Miss Featherstonehaugh straightened her tartan skirt and frowned slightly, her eyes taking on a faraway look, as if something that had just been said had triggered a distant memory. But of what she could not, or would not, reveal.

'Oh look,' cackled Claire, 'Old Miss Featherstonehaugh' – which she pronounced Feather-stone-whore – 'has just discovered a clue! What is it? Go on darling, you tell us! That you won't see another Christmas 'cos you're SO DAM' OLD?'

Denbeigh's expression did not change as he returned with a cup of tea for Miss Featherstonehaugh, but anyone who knew him would have seen his pupils dilate slightly, the only sign that he ever allowed to show that he was irritated. He remained looking so youthful because he did not move his face over often.

On the other side of the desk the Dean was tight-lipped and the vein in his temple was fluttering again. He about to say something when there was a loud bang on the door. The handle turned and in came a man in a wheelchair, being pushed by a large, handsomely built black man in a Church of England dog collar. It was immediately obvious from the direction in which the second man pushed the wheelchair – straight into the Dean's desk – that he was blind. What was not so obvious, until he spoke, was that the man in the wheelchair was deaf. His words came out in a garbled stream, only comprehensible a minute or so afterwards, by which time it was usually too late. Crunch. Tom's toes.

'Oh, great,' muttered Claire. 'Here we go; the black and white minstrel show. Hey! Sooty! Why don't ye get yerself a PROPER guide dog? Old Ironsides is no good! Couldn't find 'is way out of a PAPER BAG!'

The coloured man turned and sniffed the air.

'I smell something rotten,' he said, in a biblically deep voice.

'Would you like a cup of tea, Vicar?' asked Denbeigh.

'WOULD YOU LIKE A CUP OF TEA, VICAR?' imitated Claire. 'Never mind about him, but I bloody well would like a cup. Only fix us a proper cuppa, will you, Denbeigh? And do it properly this time. Milk and three sugars in before the tea! And I like to be able to trot a mouse across the top!'

There was a volcanic silence.

Miss Featherstonehaugh began making some little wet gasping sounds, as if experiencing the onset of an asthma attack. Her eyes

23

were fixed on Lord Denbeigh, who had turned and was looking at Claire with undisguised loathing. She stopped and turned and looked at them all with an expression that Tom could not place, but knew to be false.

'Oh, go on with you all,' she said. 'I'm only TEASING.'

4

A welcome, of sorts . . .

The Dean's party was over.

'I'll show you to your room now, if I may, Tom, and then doubtless you should like to get on to the New Library, eh? See if young Alice is there?'

Nothing further was said of what had just happened. Before the Dean had managed to call a halt to the proceedings, Claire had also managed to insult those who had arrived late: Wilfred Drover, the Lecturer in Police Procedure (whom she called a 'fat old whoopsie'); Dr Amanda Burrows, senior Lecturer in Forensics ('a tight-arse with not enough grey matter to fill an egg cup'); and the Matron (whom she taunted for having 'a mostly dead family' – something Tom understood was a bad thing to say even before everyone in the room blanched and Matron fled in tears).

They left the Dean's room in silence and walked across the winter gardens – a conservatory, barely warmer than the air outside, its brick-built beds full of strong-smelling pelargoniums and bare-branched fig trees. On the way, their feet echoing on the oak floor, the Dean pointed out some of the other rooms as they passed. Tom recognised a few names on the doors.

'Now this is your room,' he said, striding ahead to remove a name label from the brass bracket on one of the doors. Wormwood, supposed Tom. The Dean took a key from his jacket at the same time as he pocketed the label – a move requiring some dexterity – and fitted it into the lock. He fumbled for a second, a puzzled frown creeping over his face, before removing the key and studying it as if it might reveal something. He was about to try it again when the door opened as if of its own accord and they were hit by an icy wall of freezing air.[3] The Dean took a step forward into the room and then, once he had seen inside, a step back in surprise.

'Oh my word!'

The room, which Tom was beginning to think of as Wormwood's, whoever he might have been, had been carelessly, but thoroughly, searched: the furniture had been overturned, the carpet ripped up, the curtains torn down and drawers upended. Books spilled from their shelves and some of the pictures had been smashed. Over all the debris lay sheaves of paper from the drawers and piles of dirty kapok from the slashed furniture. One thin neo-Gothic window stood open and the bitter draught made everything flutter as if in a state of violated shock.

The Dean picked his way through the mess and closed the window with a leaden bang.

'Wait!' said Tom, wondering for a second if this were some test of basic technique. Snow outside and an open window meant only one thing: footprints. Tom joined the Dean by the window and ran a finger over the lead frame around the latch. Just as he thought: scratched and bent. A screwdriver, probably. He pushed it open. He vaulted lightly onto the window ledge, landing on the tips of his toes.

'Tom, I say—' began the Dean, meaning him to be careful. Tom peered out. Whoever had climbed through the window had

3 More confusion over temperatures there, but I am wondering if it really matters?

done so with difficulty. A dense hedge of spotted laurel had grown up around the window, making it difficult to get in or out, but at the same time providing good cover while one did so. Beyond was a short stretch of grass and then some kind of side road. Tom could see the roofs of a line of parked cars. He ducked under the top of the window and leaped out across the laurel to land in a roll on the frozen verge on the other side. He was on his feet in seconds, brushing the slush from his suit. He stared about him for a few seconds, frowning.

'Tom? Can you see anything?'

It was the disembodied voice of the Dean from beyond the hedge.

Tom couldn't see anything, for there was nothing to be seen, only a virgin expanse of snow[4]. The cars must belong to Fellows of the College, thought Tom: an Austin Seven, a flame-red Ferrari, a tuk-tuk and, propped against one of those old-fashioned bull-nosed Citroën vans, a tandem bicycle. Just as he might have expected.

He looked up at the window again. There was no way the thief could have gone upwards, surely? Onto the next window ledge and from there onto the roof? It was possible. There was a drain-pipe nearby, but only a fully trained circus acrobat could have made the leap. Tom stood for a while, remembering the first and most easily recalled rule of detection: once you have ruled out the impossible, whatever remains, however improbable, must be the truth. He studied the lichen that clung to the pipe. There were indeed marks, but the gap between the wall and the pipe was so narrow only the thinnest of fingers could have fitted. A child perhaps? But

---

4 Snow might suggest innocence and optimism here. Or it might not. We'll have to see.

no. No child could be that strong. A midget then? A circus midget? Why not?

If this were from the Golden Age of the Genre, then the next step would have been to find a copy of the local paper. No doubt he would have discovered an advert for a visiting troupe, the importance of which only he would guess and later reveal to the assembled cast. A circus was the perfect symbol here: playing on our fear of outsiders, our fear of the exotic, and, of course, one's now unspoken racist fear of gypsies. Oh, it had all been so easy in the past.

Tom turned and began walking back towards a door on his right, when something made him stop dead in his tracks. Perhaps it was his imagination? He was sure he had seen something, though; a blur of motion. In one of the windows on the fourth floor of the main house – a face at the window, perhaps? Watching, but not wanting to be seen. Tom stopped, startled, and counted again. One-two three four five. It was the fifth floor and yet . . . He distinctly remembered walking up to his room with the Matron. His room was on the fourth floor; he was sure there were no steps up to another floor above his own.

5

But then a ghastly surprise . . .

Tom was beginning to wonder where all this would end. The worst thing – or one of them, at any rate – was not having someone with whom to talk; someone off whom he could bounce ideas. It had been Serena, of course, but that had ended along with, it must be said, her. Unless he could find someone else to bounce ideas off, to humanise himself, then all his thoughts would remain internalised. No one liked a detective who spoke to themselves, and dialogue was so much easier on the eye.

'I need someone to talk to,' said Tom, aloud, to himself. It was a risk. That was the beauty of Serena. She knew when to ask the right questions, how to explain his more hare-brained theories and put him right when it came to all those all-too-human lacunae that made him the sleuth he hoped to become. Without her, he would be just another detective, too young to listen to classical music or nibble cheese or play the violin. He would dabble with cocaine, of course, but that was something else.

When Tom had finally retraced his steps back to his study, the Dean was pale-faced, but exertion – or anger – had brought a flush to both cheeks. He had managed to right some of the furniture and gather some of the sheets of paper together.

'There's not much we can do about all that,' he said, pointing a foot at the kapok that now lay about in drifts. 'But I'll get Symmonds – he's the handyman – to come and clear the rest up. See if he can't roust out some new cushions and whatnot while he's about it. Come on, let's leave this. There's nothing for us here, I'm sure. We'll go and see the library. See if Alice has arrived.'

Soon they were crossing the Old Quad, leaving tracks in the thin snow on the gravel, just as it was getting dark and the lights were beginning to come on. Cuff College never looked more beautiful than at this time of day.

'It's just so bloody amateurish,' the Dean was complaining. 'That's what annoys me most, Tom. Apart from all the mess, of course. We try to teach people to do this sort of thing properly, so that no one even knows their room has been searched, and then someone comes along and destroys the place. Attila the Hun couldn't have made more mess if he had tried. It must have been some outsider – some bloody low-life. An Italian or a Cockney perhaps.'

It was interesting that the Dean would not offer an apology for the ransacking, or speculate upon its motives. In truth, Tom had not taken it personally. Whoever it was had been looking for something not of his, but of Wormwood's. But what, though? That was just one question. Who was Wormwood, for a start? Why had he gone and where was he now? And who had carved those awful words in the door? And who had run away down the stairs? And who was it in room 113? And was there a way to the fifth floor? And, if so, where was it and what – or who – lay up there?

And was there a circus in town? He had still not forgotten the midget acrobat.

'Dean? Is there by any chance a circus in town at the moment?' The Dean paused in mid-stride and looked at him quizzically.

'A circus?' he said. 'No. Or, at least, not that I know of. Why? Are you a fan?'

'No. Not really. I just—'

'Ah here we are,' interrupted the Dean.

The New Library was a handsome building of the same honey-coloured stone as the main building, but with taller windows. It had been built after the Old Library burned down, some time in the 19th century, and inside it smelled of oak, leather book bindings and dust. The floor was of intricate parquet planks and the shelves, as one might expect, were full of leather-bound books. It had changed since Tom's day, though, and many of the books were in gaudy dust jackets. A great pile of unsorted books lay on one of the oak tables. The Dean picked one up and read the jacket

'*Slash and Burn*. What a title. Part of the new "STD pathologist" school. Hmm.' He tossed the book back on the pile.

'But we've got to keep up, you see, Tom. It was all very well in my day: we used to get a couple of new books a week, all of them set in English villages or Oxford Colleges. You knew where to put the books in those days, and where to find them later on when you needed them. Culinary detectives went on one shelf, over there, you see? Couples on another. It changed a bit as the Americans caught on and we had a few more sub-genres to deal with but it was essentially the same: disableds over there, short fat detectives up there, with a cross-reference to plumbers over there, do you remember? Nowadays this place looks more like a publisher's warehouse than a library. Do you know, we now have an entire section dedicated to what we have to call Canine American detectives? Sniffer dogs. Bloody hell.'

There was a noise from the office behind him.

'Aha,' said the Dean, shooting up his eyebrows and glancing at Tom knowingly. 'Perhaps it is Alice, eh? Let's go and see.'

Tom felt his chest clench again. Alice Appleton. Until he had met Serena, no other woman had really existed for Tom in quite the same way as Alice. They had met at the College and had from the first been inseparable. The Dean had had great hopes for them and Tom's memories of their time together were, until that horrible last year, golden. He could remember them walking along the banks of the river in the lemony winter sunlight, arm in arm, each of them struggling to get a word in edgeways in their desire to share and communicate. They spent long afternoons in the Tea Shoppe, on Musgrave Street, reading and re-reading Golden Age detective fiction in preparation for their Finals.

Their rivalry had been perfect until Alice had gained a double-starred first and her thesis, *A Perfect Expression of Terroir: Vineyards, Phantasmagorias and the Amateur Sleuth*, had reached the *New York Times* bestseller list under the title *The Noble Rot*. That had been the end of their friendship. Although her book – an if-only-I-had-known whodunit set in the *caves* of a château featuring an aristocratic, fine-wine-making sleuth called Baron Regis de Peyton-Grandeville – had been dedicated to him, Tom had been unable to overcome his envy. Filled with an unconquerable resentment, he had, against his best hopes, offended her so badly at the party for the book's launch that they had separated on bad terms. He had not seen her since. Her second Peyton-Grandeville book, *Phylloxera Vastatrix*, had been too clever to do very well and Tom had been glad that it had been dedicated not to him, but to their Supervisor. It was now a cult classic among diehard crime-fiction fans for its sophisticated handling of the Locked-room Lecture, which Tom admitted was brilliant, but still—

Since then Alice had written no more books. Tom had always wondered why.

The Dean knocked on the office door and, receiving no answer, gave it a gentle push. A frown puckered his brow. A sense of *déjà vu* gripped Tom. The Dean seemed to sniff the air and then stopped dead.

'Tom?' he said, his voice flat. 'Come in here, will you?'

Tom had already followed him in and the tension he had been feeling at the prospect of meeting Alice had vanished, only to be replaced by something else, something altogether more terrible. The office was ordinary: two desks and chairs of good quality, a whole wall of small drawered filing cabinets for library cards, a microfiche machine and a computer terminal with a bulky monitor. Various flyers were pinned to a cork noticeboard and there was a kettle and the wherewithal with which to make tea and coffee on a side table.

But there was something wrong with the room. It was not what he could *see* that was wrong: it was what he could *smell*. It was as if he had a copper coin in his mouth. He exchanged a look with the Dean. They both knew what it meant.

Blood.

The Dean shifted his weight and began walking very slowly towards the back of the office, the floorboards gently creaking. Tom watched. Then the Dean stopped, glanced down behind the furthest desk and closed his eyes. Tom stepped forward just as the Dean stepped back and they stood for a second, almost but not quite, touching. Tom flinched and turned away.

The body was laid out apparently peacefully on its back, its heels together and a serene expression on its face.

'Oh, my word,' said the Dean quietly. 'And now I don't suppose she will ever finish her paper on *The Performative Distortion of the Role of the Father-in-Law in Andrew Saville's* Bergerac and the Jersey Rose.'

Claire Morgan's face in repose had sunk back to the ears,

exposing those teeth – corn nuts, Tom now remembered, which were not a Spanish snack – in a ghastly grin. Her monocle, still clutched between her brow and cheek, was cracked into a star, and from her ample chest stood a spear.

6

A challenge . . .

'Poor Claire,' said the Dean. 'Although I can't say it comes as much of a surprise.'

'An assegai,' Tom said, nearly reaching out to touch the shaft of the spear.

'Mmm,' said the Dean.

'No, gentlemen, not an assegai, I think.'

It was a thin voice that came from behind their shoulders. They both turned quickly. A man stood at the door of the office clutching a pile of books. He was wearing a heavy tweed cape (what is it about amateur detectives and tweed, wondered Tom) and his beak-nosed face was as thin as a blade. His shoulders were the narrowest Tom had ever seen, his head shaped like a marrow standing on end and his hair slicked down on either side, as if with Dickensian bear's grease. He was pure intellect; a man of the ratiocinative school, ventured Tom absently.

'Oh, God. Professor Wikipedia,' muttered the Dean, rolling his eyes, but yielding some authority to the new arrival. 'What is it, then?'

'Or, rather, it *is* an assegai,' answered the strange man, 'but not what this young man means by the term.'

The Dean was in no mood to make introductions.

'Well, what does he mean by the term?'

'When he – and I assume this is the new Lecturer in Transgression and Pathology: height six foot two and three quarters; one hundred and ninety-six and a half pounds in weight; optimum Quetelet index; early thirties; hair cut by a Turkish barber somewhere in northeast London using the number-six setting on clippers that were made in Germany, possibly by the Kuno Moser company; average-number wool worsted jacket, woven in Huddersfield from Australian merino sheep, cut somewhere behind Oxford Street in London by a man with slight astigmatism in his right eye and the first sign of rheumatism in the fingers of his left hand, using a pair of scissors made in Sheffield but sharpened by a man from what was previously Austro-Hungary able to speak five languages, none of them English—'

'For God's sake, Wikipedia.'

'Furthermore, he has recently experienced a stressful bereavement, but when he – slightly dehydrated and a novice practitioner of the Alexander technique; right arm around the wicket; a decent cook; moderate drinker (by which I mean he does not drink very much, not that he is a drinker and a moderate); early interest in philately replaced by ornithology and bicycles – employs the term 'assegai', he is referring to the spear that Shaka the Zulu developed in the early part of the 19th century, and which his impis generally used as a stabbing weapon in close-quarter combat. He has, as is usual with men his age, watched too many films.'

The Dean sighed impatiently but the new man went on.

'More correctly the term 'assegai', or 'assagai', originally from the Berber 'zaġāyah' for 'spear', via the French 'azagaie' and the Spanish 'azagaya', which more accurately comes from the Arabic 'az-zaġāyah', is a weapon for throwing or hurling, usually some light spear or javelin made from wood and with an iron tip.'

'Well, exactly,' interrupted the Dean, pointing to the spear that stuck out of Claire's chest.

The man stepped around the desk with precise steps. He bent down and studied the spear rather than Claire. Tom wondered if he had actually noticed that it was stuck in a dead body.

'This assegai is, I suspect, judging by the length of its shaft and the *mopane* wood used, and look here – the way the blade is attached – yes, definitely this assegai is almost certainly turn of the century before last, from one of the tribes on the western limits of South Africa, perhaps the *Batlhaping* or the *Bakgalagadi* or perhaps the *Buhurutsi* or *Barolong*. I will not be able to tell for certain until I see the tip of the blade.'

'I'll ring the police,' said Tom reaching for the phone on the Librarian's desk.

'Wait!' The Dean caught Tom's wrist in a surprisingly powerful grip and held it firm.

'Let's just think about this for a minute, shall we?' he said quietly.

Tom almost laughed.

'You're surely not going to suggest we *don't* call the police, are you?'

A silence followed. All three men looked at one another. Both the Dean and this new man were excited.

'Tom,' began the Dean, talking to him, but looking at the arrival. 'This sort of thing comes along only once in a generation. There is a chance to prove something here. Whose methods work best? The police, with their size 13 boots and flashing blue lights and stupid questions from men who can't even write "bum" on a wall, or ours, with recourse to experimental scientific methods and recondite knowledge such as Wikipedia's here.'

Now Professor Wikipedia introduced himself with a long,

thin, tepid hand. Tom shook it. It was like gripping a dead eel.

'Professor Aldous Wikipedia,' he smiled, revealing two rows of tiny sharp teeth. 'Reader in Scientific Detection and Pro-Vice Chancellor of the University. Pleased to meet you. The Dean is, if anything, understating the case here, Tom, if I may call you that?'

Tom nodded.

'You see,' continued Wikipedia. 'With all this terrorism in the headlines, we have been losing ground to thrillers. You know the sort: government agencies, global conspiracies, multinationals and unknowable biochemical Jihadis with their dirty bombs lurking in every distant cave you care to mention. Death has become random now. It's all suicide bombers and Operation Wrath of God. We need to get back to the personal again, Tom, where individuals can make a difference.

'It is a strange literary fact, not wholly germane to our conversation, true, but worth noting nonetheless, that those people who vote 'to get the government off their backs' always want to read about the Government intruding in other people's lives: an intrusion that usually takes the shape of a Chinook helicopter overhead and the muzzle of a machine gun in your face.'

He turned to the body of Claire with a zealot's gleam in his eye.

'This, on the other hand, is *a body in the library*!'

Had Wikipedia or the Dean been younger or American, they might have whooped or done a dance of victory here. Their elation was almost sexual. Tom felt suddenly uncomfortable, the odd man out.

'So, Dean,' Wikipedia said. 'What you are proposing is a competition between us and the modern state. Whoever solves the crime first wins? Nothing but intellectual pride at stake. Rather unfair, don't you think? Harharhar.'

He had an unpleasant forced laugh that cut itself off dead.

'The police must, of course, remain within the law,' the Dean continued, 'and they don't know they are in a competition, but they have far greater resources at their disposal.'

Wikipedia rubbed his hands together. Tom could hardly take his eyes off them: it was like watching snakes writhe.

'Tom, you ring the police,' suggested Wikipedia. 'Tell them we have found A Body in the Library. They'll never believe you, of course. I'll have a look at this spear and the aforementioned body, if I may.'

Wikipedia squatted down and touched her forehead.

'Still warm,' he murmured to the Dean, who squatted next to him. Tom, using the phone on the desk, got through to the police station at St Aldgate's. It took him a full five minutes to persuade someone he was not wasting police time. Eventually the police agreed to come. He put the phone down and joined the two men.

'Now,' said the Dean. 'The first question we have to ask ourselves is whether Claire had any enemies.'

'Enemies?' said Wikipedia 'Good Lord! Did she have any *friends*?'

'Yes, well, it doesn't make it any easier,' agreed the Dean. 'We shall have to draw up a longlist. Tom? Grab a pencil and paper, will you? We should write this down. I am thinking first of Yardley, who hated her for not using his books on her course, and whom she regularly teased about his speech impediment. Then there is Mrs Robinson, who hates – hated I should say, dear God – her because she was always so rude about her cooking. Then there is Rex, of course, whom she thought elderly and homosexualist – a fatal combination – and then poor dear Celia, who so hated Claire for telling Rex about all those previous engagements. Then there is Miss Featherstonehaugh, whom she ridiculed for being A Bit

Like Miss Marple, but who might be thought of as being a touch on the frail side for fighting with spears, which might, I suppose, rule her out, but then there is Lord Denbeigh, who detested her because she was c-o-m-m-o-n.'

The Dean spelled the word out, peering around him as he did, as if just saying it were enough to evoke the forces of darkness.

'As good a reason as any to murder someone,' chimed Wikipedia. 'Happens all the time.'

Tom scribbled away.

'Then there is poor Father Dennis,' continued the Dean, 'whom she persuaded that people had been lying to him all his life and that he was not, in fact, black but a Native American Indian. He might, now that I come to think of it, be the most natural person to be throwing a spear about the place, were it not for the fact that he is blind. Again, that is something that might just rule him out, unless he did it in cahoots with Thorneycroft, whose deafness has only served to enhance his sense of touchiness, and who hated Claire for calling him Ironsides and 'The-seeing-eye-dog-of-Tonto' in that absurd cod 'Red Injun' voice she used to put on, although to be fair, this part of the Library is not equipped for wheelchair access, and so that might rule him out too.'

'I sense we are getting somewhere,' said Wikipedia, wiggling his eyebrows.

'And then there is Drover, whom she was always calling fat but who thought of himself as merely portly and who hated her because she would not come on the Gay Rights march in London last year and who thought she was a hypocrite for not publicly admitting her love for Dr Burrows, whose marriage she had ruined by stalking her so incessantly, even while she was married to her own husband, who then committed suicide, but whose sister, Nurse Lane, is the Matron and whom you, Tom, saw earlier this afternoon. How did she seem?'

'Oh,' said Tom, a little lost. 'Fine, I think.'

'That's all very well,' said Wikipedia. 'They were all in the College at the time of the death and they all had a motive, if not the means, but it is this spear that really intrigues me.'

Tom sensed that something had changed. He had been sure they were right to concentrate on the list of people with the motives and perhaps the means to kill Claire, and that they ought to consult the porters in their cabin to find out if anyone had come or gone through the gates in the last couple of hours. Yet here he was, having to concentrate on the spear. He was being corralled in a direction he did not necessarily want to go. This was the sort of thing that only usually happened in films.

'Wait a minute—' he began. 'The police will be here any minute. They won't want you to disturb the—'

But Wikipedia had wrapped his silk handkerchief around the shaft of the spear and pulled it from Claire's body with the sound of someone removing a spade from wet sand. Tom looked away as he wiped the sticky blood from its vicious tip.

'Hmmm,' he said. 'Very interesting. Look at this. It is extra-ordinarily ornate. Too ornate for the *Batlhaping*. It must have been made by the *Bamangwato* of what we used to call Northern Bechuanaland, now Botswana. They were the finest metalworkers in southern Africa, you know. Even then the detail is really remark-able. This must have been made for a king. Look at the decor-ation here. Very ornate. Very rare. I know of only one like this in existence: in the National Museum in Gaborone in Botswana.'

'Who could have got hold of a spear like this?' asked the Dean. Tom was, despite himself, interested in this development. A rare antique as a murder weapon had a nice, familiar chime.

'Obviously it's a message,' Wikipedia said, looking at the Dean with a significant leer.

'You don't think?' The Dean looked aghast at some fresh possibility. Wikipedia nodded, enjoying the gravity of the moment.

'Have you told him?' he asked, tilting his strange-shaped head towards Tom. Tom could see he was being drawn into something else again here. The atmosphere changed and it seemed as if the lights had dimmed around them. For a moment he managed to forget that at their feet was the bulky body of his erstwhile Head of Department.

'What?' Tom asked, speaking in a whisper.

'Tom, the police will be here soon and so we do not have much time. There has been some trouble here at the College in the last few months. You may have heard something? And not just here. All over the place. It started with just the odd slip-up. A case unsolved, unresolved. Once or twice this is all right – terribly po-mo – but it has been happening too often and people do not like it. The reading public like to be reassured that, through whatever means, disorder is contained and transgression punished.'

'You see,' took over Wikipedia, 'too many of our alumni are reporting mistakes or, worse, blank walls, dead ends. At first we thought it might mean increasingly cunning criminals, increasingly interesting Crime Fiction, but then we started getting the letters.'

'Letters?'

'In the post. From all over the world. Someone is trying to undermine us, Tom. Trying to catch us out, trying to show that the current crop of literary detectives are no good; unsettling them and destroying their confidence. There have been cases of them acting strangely: taking to drink, or giving it up. Someone is challenging us. This,' he held up the spear, 'is just another sign. It is a summons. One of us needs to get out to Botswana and find out what all this is about.'

'But—' began Tom.

The Dean held up a hand.

'Tom, even to so much as suggest there may be alternative courses of action, such as waiting for the police, even to suggest we may be wrong about this, is to lose the plot; lose the game; lose the audience; the reader. Surely you know that?'

This was one of the Basic Rules of the Genre, something Tom had known in theory almost all his life. He had not realised how hard it was to rub up against it in real life.

'We have a contact in Botswana, of course. Delicious Ontoaste; class of '74. You may have heard of her?'

Of course Tom had heard of Delicious Ontoaste. She had been one of the College's great successes of the last ten years. Despite having started with a minor academic publisher, she had become a word-of-mouth bestseller – the best kind of bestseller.

'And you want me to go, don't you? Because of my father?'

Wikipedia nodded sharply. Then he tossed the spear up in the air, its point missing Tom's eye by an inch, caught it by the shaft and plunged it back into the wound in Claire's chest with a glutinous squeal. The body gave a kind of a sigh and deflated.

'Always wanted to do that,' he said and smiled.

At that point they heard a voice at the door – a curious high-pitched squeak – and together all three whirled around. Alice Appleton. Tom's first sight of her after ten years was just as she twisted at her knees and fainted to the floor in a heap.

'Oh dear,' said the Dean.

Part II

The 11 O'Clock Moral Dilemma

CHAPTER ONE

The Tiny White Aeroplane and the man in the uniform of the Botswana Postal Service both make an appearance.

Mma Delicious Ontoaste, redoubtable founder of <u>The Best Detective Agency in the World Ever! No. 2</u>, was sitting beneath a striped parasol outside the café at the Sir Seretse Kharma International Airport in Gaborone. On the table in front of her was a mug of foaming bush tea and the sky above her was of the colour it usually assumed at ten o'clock in the morning: clear, blue and cloudless. It was a good sky, Mma Ontoaste sometimes thought; the best sky in the world, stretching all the way to the horizon of the best country in the world, and she was the best woman in the world, sitting there, still with that mug of foaming bush tea, still thinking strange thoughts, except that today Mma Ontoaste was not thinking strange thoughts about the sky. Mma Ontoaste was thinking strange thoughts about the tiny white aeroplane and the Very Important Person on board whom she had come to the airport to meet.

It had begun a few days before, when Mma Ontoaste had been sitting in her office on Merchistone Drive, sipping bush tea from her own mug, the one her dear late daddy – that good man – had passed on to her, and listening to her new assistant, Mma Murakami – that good woman – as she typed very quickly in the grass hut next door. Outside nothing except the air moved. It was one of those long hot African days, when there seemed to be no escape from the heat. The sun beat down on the grass roof of the hut and the cattle sought out the shade of the acacia tree. The red soil bounced the heat back up and it seemed as if between them the sun and the earth had declared war on anything cool and green and living.

Behind the steady clatter of Mma Murakami's typewriter, Mma Ontoaste could hear a radio playing some jazz music. It was Mma Murakami's radio, a leather-encased Roberts radio, with a wire clothes-hanger in place of the original aerial, which Mma Ontoaste assumed had been broken off in some accident or other in the past. Ordinarily jazz was the outward sign of deep inner corruption or incurable evil, of course and, had Mma Ontoaste known that her new assistant Mma Murakami not only had a radio, but that she also listened to jazz while she typed, then it is doubtful that Mma Ontoaste would have given Mma Murakami the job in the first place, even if she had, as she claimed, got 98 per cent in her final exam at the Napier Secretarial College.

But lessons were there to be learned, were they not, and once her old assistant, Mma Pollosopresso, had revealed herself to be a bad woman, who would go so far as to blow up her employer's tiny white van with explosives made from a half cup of sugar which she must have hoarded while she had been working at the Detective Agency and some fertiliser that she would have borrowed from the orphan farm, well then Mma Ontoaste had had no choice but to ask her to leave the Detective Agency and employ Mma Murakami in her place.

And it was just as Mma Ontoaste was sitting on the chair on

the veranda of the grass hut, sipping more bush tea, and looking out across the yard at the pumpkin patch and the melons and the other nameless shrubs that filled the space, thinking of how much she loved it all, that the man wearing the uniform of the Botswana Postal Service, a smart uniform, with blue shorts and a white shirt, had knocked at the gate of the stock fence and greeted her modestly.

'Mma.'

'Rra,' she had said, getting to her feet to meet her visitor and to show him to a chair in the old Botswana custom. The man in the uniform of the Botswana Postal Service had looked puzzled for a second, but he had readily accepted her offer of bush tea and a slice of cake and this pleased Mma Ontoaste. So few people these days had time to stop and talk. Her beloved father, Pepe, was of the mind that anything that could not be solved over a cup of bush tea was probably not worth solving anyway. In this he was probably right, if you believed, as Mma Ontoaste did, that people were basically good, but, sadly, just a little bit thick. They needed to be told what to think and what to do and here they were in luck, because, apart from bush tea, thick slices of richly fruited cake and her husband, Mr JPS Spagatoni, that good man, as well as numerous friends and the cows that her father – that other good man – had left her in his will, Mma Ontoaste loved nothing more than telling people what to do.

'Now, Rra,' she said. 'What can I do for you?'

'Mma,' he replied, using the respectful greeting that, along with his polite acceptance of her offer of the chair and the thick slice of cake and the bush tea, confirmed him to be a good man, 'I have a telegram for you.'

In one hand he held out a brown envelope with Mma Ontoaste's name and address written upon it.

'Oh Rra, a telegram!' Mma Ontoaste clapped her hands together. 'I am so happy! You are so clever! However did you find me?'

The man in the uniform of the Botswana Postal Service pointed to the name and the address written on the envelope in black ink. True it was not handwritten, but printed rather, which was a pity. Mma Ontoaste was not against progress or change, of course. Just look at Botswana. Had not that good country changed since that hot night all those years ago when the fireworks failed to ignite and which seemed to augur ill for Independence, etc etc?

And yet change was not always a good thing, Mma Ontoaste sometimes thought, especially if it led to people becoming cold and selfish as they were in South Africa, Zimbabwe, Zambia, Namibia, Angola, Mozambique, Malawi and, of course, the Democratic Republic of Congo. She could have gone on listing the countries where people were also lazy and stupid, and full of malevolence, but Mma Ontoaste was one of those people who preferred to emphasise the positive.

'Oh Rra!' she exclaimed. 'I must show this to Mma Murakami. She will be so excited. She is my new assistant. She passed her exams at the Napier Secretarial College with 98 per cent.'

'Oh, that is good, Mma. Napier Secretarial College is a very fine college. Your new assistant must be very clever. Ninety-eight per cent is better than 97 per cent.'

'Exactly, Rra. I am glad to hear you say that. I had to ask my last assistant to leave because she only got 97 per cent in her final exams. And then she blew up my tiny white van. Can you imagine that?'

'Oh, Mma. Are you sure it was her?'

With that the man in the uniform of the Botswana Postal Service wiped the cake crumbs from his lips with the back of his hand. Mma Ontoaste was taken aback. This was not the old Botswana way. Wiping one's mouth with the back of one's hand was the rudest thing a man could do and it occurred to Mma Ontoaste that the man who was dressed in the uniform of the Botswana Postal Service was not perhaps from Botswana, but rather Nigeria, where they were known to be very rude and selfish and constantly wiping crumbs from their mouths with the backs of their hands. Yes. The more she thought of it, the more certain Mma Ontoaste became that this man in the uniform of the Botswana Postal Service was not from Botswana but from some other country, somewhere else. The question then was why had he got a job in the Botswana Postal Service in the first place?

'Rra?' Mma Ontoaste started. 'May I ask you a question?'

For a second the man in the uniform of the Botswana Postal Service stared at her but then, before Mma Ontoaste could ask her question, he snatched up the remaining slice of cake and jammed it in his mouth before bolting across the yard and out through the gate in the stock fence, his postal bag swinging wildly behind him.

Well, thought Mma Ontoaste, still sitting in her chair, does that not take the biscuit!

Mma Delicious Ontoaste took the envelope that the man in the uniform of the Botswana Postal Service had left on the table and she opened it with a letter knife that her father – that dear good man – had left her, commemorating his visit to Las Vegas. She was surprised by the contents. A single sheet of thin paper stamped in a long line of capital letters. Mma Ontoaste read the letters that together made up a series of words:

TO MMA ONTOASTE STOP OWNER OF THE BEST DETECTIVE AGENCY IN THE WORLD EVER EXCLAMATION MARK NO. 2 STOP TOM HURST LECTURER IN

TRAN AND PATH ON WAY TO BOTSWANA STOP URGENT HELP NEEDED STOP SENSITIVE MATTER STOP MURDER MOST FOUL STOP MALICE AFORETHOUGHT STOP ARRIVES GABORONE FLIGHT SA 235/1763 06/01 STOP. DEAN CUFF COLLEGE

'Well,' exclaimed Mma Ontoaste. 'What can that be about, I wonder?'

CHAPTER TWO

Mma Murakami does not answer the door when Mma Ontoaste knocks on it and Mma Ontoaste thinks this is very rude. Then, a bit later, she has a disagreeable surprise as a new bride loses and then, to be fair, finds, her new husband but not without having had a fright on the way.

Mma Ontoaste sat for a second on the veranda and she thought that this would be the perfect thing to talk to Mma Murakami about over a cup of bush tea. It would be their first case together and it promised to be an especially interesting case too, and so Mma Ontoaste knocked on the door of Mma Murakami's office, the implication of this being that she wanted to come in. But Mma Murakami was typing loudly and still listening to jazz music on her new transistor radio and so she did not hear the owner of <u>The Best Detective Agency in the World Ever! No. 2</u> knocking on the door and, after a minute, Mma Ontoaste returned to her own desk, a frown on her face.

Mma Ontoaste would be able to think about Mma Murakami's curious behaviour only after she had spoken to her husband, that good man, Mr JPS Spagatoni, over lunch at his the Salt-'n'-Sauce Scotch Chip Supper Shop on Murieston Road, or perhaps later, when the children were in bed and the sun had sunk behind the red hills and the moon hung in the old acacia tree, a time when the air was cool, a time when it was proper to sit on the veranda with a foaming mug of bush tea and talk about the events of the day.

First, though, she must go to the loo.

After that her next task would be to find out why a man who had wiped his mouth with the back of his hand and who was probably a Nigerian in the first place should have been given a job representing that fine old institution the Botswana Postal Service. Mma Ontoaste knew that in some countries, such as South Africa, Zimbabwe, Zambia, Namibia, Angola, Mozambique and Malawi, and not forgetting of course the Democratic Republic of Congo, there was such a thing as corruption, where a man such as the man who had so recently been to see her to deliver that telegram might wangle himself a job that he did not deserve simply because he had connections in high places. This would never happen in Botswana, of course, but constant vigilance was the price that needed to be paid, and so Mma Ontoaste made up her mind to go and see whomever it was in charge of the Botswana Postal Service and have the impostor exposed.

'That will be a nice job to do,' she said aloud.

It was nice to hear a voice; even if it was her own, and for a second Mma Ontoaste found that she missed the company of her former assistant, Mma Pollosopresso, whom she had had to replace with Mma Murakami after Mma Ontoaste had read of that good lady's score in her final examination from the Napier Secretarial College. Mma Ontoaste had now twice been given cause to regret her decision to let her former assistant leave. The first time had been when she had been walking along the road and seen a painter painting a sign for a new Detective Agency – <u>The Only Detective</u>

Agency You Will Ever Need Ever! No. 3, – that Mma Pollosopresso was trying to set up in Gaborone.

Mma Ontoaste put the telegram aside and thought back to her time at Cuff College, from which she had graduated without any great expectations many years before. Although she had not enjoyed the cold[5] of that far-off country, and had missed Botswana and its people while she had been away, she knew that she would be happy to help this man whom the Dean was sending. She would be able to show him the glories of Botswana: the bush, the grass huts, the other stuff, but most of all she would show him the simple decency of the people of Botswana. He would find that there were still parts of the world where people were in touch with the earth and their own souls.

The rest of the day was rather quiet at The Best Detective Agency in the World Ever! No. 2 and there were no appointments booked at all. All that Mma Ontoaste had in mind was to sit on her veranda and sip bush tea until the afternoon was sufficiently cool enough for her to consider walking to the main telegram office in Gaborone to see if she could not get to the bottom of the mystery of the man in the uniform of the Botswana Postal Service. She hoped that the man would be sent back to where he came from: Nigeria. Yes. It was definitely Nigeria. Only a Nigerian would wipe away crumbs with the back of his hand. Mma Ontoaste thought to herself that the man probably hawked and spat occasionally and that he probably practised witchcraft or played football.

But it was when Mma Ontoaste awoke from her afternoon nap, thinking it might be cool enough for her to go and get the Nigerian, as she had come to think of him, sacked that she found

5 Again! But what does it *mean*?

an unwelcome surprise: a woman was sitting on the veranda with her head in her hands, weeping. She was a young woman of about 35, in a red dress and some other things such as shoes that she believed women wore.

Mma Ontoaste studied the Botswana sky and guessed that it must be about now that a client with a human-interest case was due and so here she was. Ordinarily in a situation such as this, Mma Ontoaste and Mma Pollosopresso might offer the lady a mug of bush tea and sit and listen to her as she told them all about her problems. After that they would have a think about what the lady had said and then, drawing on a little common sense and a modicum of human understanding, they would tell the woman what they thought she ought to do. Sometimes they did not even have to think very hard about what their client ought to do. In fact, it was often very obvious what their client ought to do from the very beginning, and that was the way that Mma Ontoaste liked it. It was, after all, why she lived in Botswana. That and all the other stuff, of course, such as the easy access to pumpkins.

'Mma, can I help you?' asked Mma Ontoaste. The lady briefly stopped sobbing to wipe her eyes and look at Mma Ontoaste.

'Oh, Mma,' she said. 'It is my husband. He has disappeared.'

'Disappeared! Oh, Mma! That is bad. Can you tell me about him? What is his name?'

'My husband's name is Machende Arimuhapwa. We have been married for only a very short time, just over a week in fact, Mma, and we live in a house further along this road towards Lobatse.'

The woman, Mma Arimuhapwa, pointed at the road that passed Mma Ontoaste's yard, the one that joined Lobatse to Gaborone.

'Oh, that is a nice address,' said Mma Ontoaste. 'Your husband sounds like a nice man, Mma.'

'Oh, he is, Mma,' replied the Mma Arimuhapwa. 'After our wedding we travelled to see his people in a village near Molepololololopole and we enjoyed ourselves very very much. His people are very kind, Mma, and we were sad to leave, but my husband has a job at a government office here in Gaborone and he does not get very much holiday.'

'I see,' said Mma Ontoaste.

'We got back from his people's place just yesterday and then this morning my husband got up and he put on a suit and a shirt and a tie, Mma, and then he took a small case with him and he kissed me on each cheek and then he left our grass hut and I have not seen him since.'

The woman started sobbing again. This was a mystery indeed.

'And was he acting strangely before he left?'

'Not at all, Mma. It was as if it were the most natural thing in the world.'

'Did you see which way he went after he had left your grass hut?'

The woman's eyes flew open and Mma Ontoaste felt she was on to something here.

'Oh Mma! That was the strange thing. I forgot about that. My husband stood for a while with three or four other men by a metal post stuck in the side of the road and they were talking only half-heartedly, as if they were waiting for something, or as if they did not know each other very well, you know, Mma? And then this great big grey motor car came along and stopped in front of them and a door opened and one by one the men went into it and then the door closed behind them with a strange hissing sound and then the car drove off.'

'I think I have seen such a vehicle,' said Mma Ontoaste.

'And I saw that above a window on the front of the car there was a sign that said 'Gaborone'. Oh Mma, whatever can it mean?'

This was a good question and, for a moment, Mma Ontoaste was stumped. Behind her the typing of Mma Murakami was getting faster than ever and Mma Ontoaste was finding it hard to concentrate.

'I will have to do some looking around, Mma, and I will let you know.'

'Don't you want to know what he looks like?' asked the woman.

'I am sorry, Mma,' replied Mma Ontoaste. 'Descriptions are of no use to me. You see, all black men look the same to me.'

The woman looked puzzled as Mma Ontoaste began to walk with her towards the stock fence. Mma Ontoaste walked Mma Arimuhapwa through the stock gate and they stood for a second by the side of the road.

'I am sure your husband will turn up, Mma. It is not uncommon that men go away for a bit every day.'

It was while Mma Ontoaste was saying this that a grey bus appeared along the road in the direction of Gaborone, heading towards them.

'Look, Mma!' cried the woman, pointing down the road over Mma Ontoaste's shoulder. Her eyes were big and round and she was clearly terrified.

'Another one of those strange cars! We must be careful that it does not eat us up alive!'

Mma Arimuhapwa turned and ran up the road away from the approaching bus, her hands waggling in the air.

'Aiyeeee!' she cried.

A sign on the front of the bus read Lobatse and just as the bus drew level with a pole in the side of the road and the fleeing Mma Arimuhapwa, it stopped. Out stepped a man wearing a suit and tie. In his hand he had a briefcase and it looked as if he had just come back from work in one of the government offices in Gaborone.

This, observed Mma Ontoaste with some satisfaction, might be the missing government office worker Machende Arimuhapwa.

CHAPTER THREE

It's moral dilemma time again! They cried.

The next morning Mma Ontoaste was wide awake in time for her
11 o'clock Moral Dilemma. She could see that an important client
had arrived and was standing waiting under the *mopane* tree. Mma
Ontoaste wondered why someone might hang about under a tree
– such a dismal spot – rather than wait in the waiting room of
the grass hut, but that was for them. Some people were just back-
ward: pig-ignorant, stuck in their ways. Mma Ontoaste could hear
Mma Murakami's jazz playing loudly now, and she began to like
what she heard.

The client who had been standing beneath the *mopane* tree
was a lady of about the same age as Mma Ontoaste, but as she
emerged from the shade and came to sit down at the proffered
chair, Mma Ontoaste could see that this lady was fat. She was
at least a size 22 and for a second Mma Ontoaste feared for her
supplies of cake. This lady looks as if she might be able to eat
me out of hut and home, thought Mma Ontoaste, and she
suddenly decided not to offer her any cake. It was as simple as
that and once she had made the decision, Mma Ontoaste felt
happy. It would be silly to waste cake on a person like this. It

would be like trying to fill Lake Victoria with bush tea.

'Mma, what can I do for you?' Mma Ontoaste asked, ignoring the slightly thirsty noises the woman was making as she slumped into the chair.

'Oh, Mma,' said the lady, 'I can see you are an old-fashioned lady and that you take the time to talk—'

Mma Ontoaste rolled her eyes and promised herself that she would buy herself a stopwatch of the sort that were used in chess matches. That way she would be able to time people as they spoke and make it very clear to them that she was the owner of The Best Detective Agency in the World Ever! No. 2, and not just some nosey old curtain twitcher with a little too much time on her hands.

'Yes, yes, Mma. Never mind all that. Time is money. What can I do for you?'

The woman was taken aback, but she carried on as best she could.

'Mma, I have a friend who is a woman who used to work as an assistant to a lady private detective but has been given the sack because the private detective thought that she had not achieved a high enough score in some secretarial exams.'

'Right,' said Mma Ontoaste wearily. 'So?'

'Well, a few weeks ago I saw a lion in my garden and I was very frightened and so my friend – the same one who is very upset, I should say – lent me a gun.'

'A gun?'

'Yes: a big black gun, full of bullets. It is, I think, big enough to stop an elephant in its tracks.'

'It sounds very dangerous, Mma.'

'It is. And yesterday my friend asked me if I could give it back to her.'

61

Mma Ontoaste sat back on her chair and looked at her client. She was trying to stifle a yawn.

'Mma,' she said. 'Why are you telling me this?'

'Because I have a problem, Mma, which I need to sort out. I am a virtuous woman, as you know, and in ordinary circumstances I should hand the gun straight back to my friend, shouldn't I?'

'Of course,' agreed Mma Ontoaste.

'But,' the lady went on. 'My friend is very unhappy about having lost her job, Mma.'

'Oh, Mma, that is very bad,' said Mma Ontoaste.

'Yes. In fact, she has gone quite crazy. You see, she feels that she was unjustly treated.'

'Injustice is a bad thing, a bad thing indeed. Your friend is right to be upset Mma.'

'Yes. I feel I should give her the gun back, Mma, but I am worried she will do something dangerous with it. She might even go after her ex-employer and shoot her in her big fat head with the gun. Twice or even three times until her ex-employer is quite dead, Mma.'

Mma Ontoaste thought for a second. After a second she knew the answer.

'You must give her the gun back, Mma. That is your duty as a virtuous woman. What your friend then does with the gun is up to her.'

The woman in the chair was silent for a minute. Then she slapped her hands on the arms of the chair and hauled herself to her feet. It was as if something had just been decided, but Mma Ontoaste could not say for sure what it was.

'Very well,' the lady said. 'I shall give her the gun tonight.'

'Good,' said Mma Ontoaste. 'And now I have to go and have some lunch. I am starving.'

Mma Ontoaste relieved the woman of 5000 Pula and then, since Mma Murakami was still hard at work and not in a position to join her for lunch, Mma Ontoaste went to find her husband, that good man, Mr JPS Spagatoni, in his chip supper shop out by the old Ulster Defence headquarters, on Murieston Road.

It was here at the Salt-'n'-Sauce Scotch Chip Supper Shop that Mr JPS Spagatoni served up the finest example of Scotch cuisine that sub-Saharan Africa had to offer. He battered everything from Mars bars to fillets of impala before dipping them into seething brown fat and, once they were cooked through, keeping them under heat lamps for as long as a week at a time and then selling them to passing drunks. He was especially proud of his deep-fried battered Pizza Calzone, which, when covered with special brown sauce and served with a solid fist of damp chips, made the perfect supper for any right-thinking person.

Too many people these days were worried about the effect such suppers might have on a human's digestion over a prolonged period of time, thought Mma Ontoaste, but her own beloved father, who had also fallen in love with the Scotch diet, had lived on such a diet until he had been taken happily, without a word of protest, at the age of 36, knowing his time was up.

It was as she was walking through the yard, with her footsteps especially firm so as to alert any snakes who were apt at this time of day to be at their most somnolent and therefore at their most dangerous, that Mma Ontoaste remembered of course that her former assistant, Mma Pollosopresso, had, in an act of vengeance that had taken Mma Ontoaste's breath away, both literally and figuratively, detonated a sizeable bomb under the tiny white van that she had driven about the streets of Gaborone ever since receiving it as a graduation present from her dear (albeit dead) daddy.

This was a pity because Mma Ontoaste had given a lot of thought to which vehicle would be suitable for a lady detective of her standing, and the tiny white van, she had decided, had been perfect. Replacing it with anything else now would be difficult. There were no detectives she could think of who rented their cars, or who just drove blue cars, say, or red cars, or yellow cars, or who changed their car with each book. Of course it was a bit of a cheap trick to give a detective the characteristic of driving a particular car, as if the choice of car might say anything more about them than their choice of shoes, but it was memorable, and that Mma Ontoaste had to admit. Mma Ontoaste tried to think of any other type of character so easily identified by their car as, for example, Inspector Morse was by his old Jaguar, or even, Heaven help us, 'Jim' Bergerac was by his Triumph.

Could she not come up with anything better than that? Mma Ontoaste wondered. She recalled her Supervisor at Cuff College advising them that their choice of vehicle was just as important as their choice of companion. And yet had Mma Ontoaste not just replaced her companion? Perhaps this could be her trick? Could she not just go down to a garage in Gaborone and buy a hybrid car?

In the meantime she would have to get a bus. But after the affair of the missing government office worker Machende Arimuhapwa, the bus company (whose motto was 'We Guarantee to Get You There Alive if at all Possible') did not instil confidence. It was as she was thinking this that her eye fell upon the small herd of cattle that her dear daddy had left her in that never-to-be-forgotten will. Would a cow do? she wondered. Could Mma Ontoaste ride a cow on her investigations? Whyever not? she thought. In many ways a cow would make an ideal mount. They were solid and dependable, much like her beloved Botswana, and one could hang things from their horns such as bags of produce one had bought from the market in Castle Terrace.

The only problem with the new plan was that Mma Ontoaste was a large woman who might very easily crush the cow to death. This was a serious problem. Mma Ontoaste could have lost some weight, of course, and there was some medical evidence to suggest that it was not healthy to be so heavily 'built', but it was good to be fat and that, as her husband Mr JPS Spagatoni, that good man, that good man who fried chips for a living, might say, was that. Some people liked modern-shaped ladies, of course, of the sort who could resist the temptation of an extra slice of cake with their bush tea in the afternoons while they were sitting and talking to old friends, but Mma Delicious Ontoaste was not one of these ladies. She was the sort of lady who knew the importance of sitting and eating and so, when she approached the herd of cows, sheltering in the shade of a *mopane* tree, she did so with consideration for the pain that she might be about to inflict upon one of their number.

CHAPTER FOUR

In which a bottle of Irn-Bru comes between a man and his wife with some quite bad consequences.

It was just as Mr JPS Spagatoni of the Salt-'n'-Sauce Scotch Chip Supper Shop on Murieston Road, Botswana's leading Scotch chip shop, was drying his hands on another piece of clean lint and watching one of the trainee fryers cut a cauliflower into individual florets for dipping in batter, that he realised that something was wrong. Mr JPS Spagatoni was a good man, but that is not to say he was a clever man, and so, although he was the best fryer of pizza Calzone suppers in the land – a fact of which he was enormously proud – it took him some moments to realise what it was that had been bothering him for the past few days. There was, he finally realised, no music.

The radio, which he had kept on the top shelf on the wall behind the counter, along with catering-sized jars of pickled eggs and boxes of spare plastic chip forks, was missing. It had been an old leather-bound Roberts transistor radio with a coat-hanger in place of an aerial, and Forth Radio had been playing in the shop for as long as Mr JPS Spagatoni could remember. Now though all he could hear was the steady buzz of the extractor fan and the low murmur of the seething oil. Where was the radio?

'Dennis?' he asked the trainee. 'Have you seen the radio? It was up there on that shelf and now it has gone.'

'No, Rra,' said Dennis. 'I have not seen the radio.'

This seemed straightforward enough. So the radio had been stolen. Thank God I am just a humble fryer of fish, thought Mr JPS Spagatoni, and not a great detective like Mma Ontoaste. She will know what to do in a case like this. Mma Ontoaste would be able to come up with a plan.

And at that moment, through the door of his chip shop Mr JPS Spagatoni, that good man, saw Mma Ontoaste arriving outside, struggling to parallel park her cow on Murieston Road.

Mr JPS Spagatoni and Mma Ontoaste had been married for three years now and in all that time, so busy had they been with foaming bush tea, errant vans, frying potato suppers and staring at the scenery that they had spent not one minute alone together, and so no one in Botswana, that good country, could say for certain what they did when they were alone, or comment on the state of their relationship, and this, perhaps, was a good thing. There was too much of that sort of thing in the world. After all, whose business was it what they did when they were alone? Mma Ontoaste and Mr JPS Spagatoni had shown that it was possible to glean an idea of someone's character without intruding on their most private or intimate moments. But no one who knew them even in passing could resist speculating on what really lay between them and, in the vacuum, the theories were legion.

While Mma Ontoaste ate a pizza Calzone supper with extra salt and sauce, Mr JPS Spagatoni told her about the missing radio. Mma Ontoaste listened in silence, her eye drifting over the entertainment section of the newspaper, and when Mr JPS Spagatoni had finished he stepped back and waited to hear what her plan would be.

'There is a circus in town, you know, Rra? It has come all the way from the North Pole!'

'Oh the North Pole is a long way away, Mma,' said Dennis. 'I hope the polar bears are not suffering too much in our climate. All that fur is not good.'

'But what about the radio, Mma?' asked Mr JPS Spagatoni.

There was a silence for a few seconds. Mma Ontoaste seemed to have returned to the paper, where she was reading a story about a break-in at the Botswana National Museum that had occurred some weeks before. After a second she looked up. She had not been listening to Mr JPS Spagatoni or Dennis at all.

'Rra,' she said. 'Can I have a bottle of Irn-Bru?'

'A bottle of Irn-Bru?' asked Mr JPS Spagatoni, stunned for a moment. Mma Ontoaste did not drink Irn-Bru. She drank bush tea.

'Is there something wrong, Mma?' he asked.

'No, Rra. I just fancied a change.'

A change? First there was the way in which Mma Ontoaste had asked Mma Pollosopresso to leave. Then there was the cow inconsiderately parked in the sun outside (and getting a ticket, Mr JPS Spagatoni could see, through the door of his grass-hutted chip shop) and now Irn-Bru instead of bush tea. No one doubted Irn-Bru's revitalising qualities, of course, but still: this was not the Mma Ontoaste whom Mr JPS Spagatoni knew and loved. He blamed this new assistant.

'Well Mma, what about my radio?' he asked. 'Have you had any further thoughts on that?'

'Rra,' she said, tipping her head back and draining the bottle of orange liquid in three large gulps, so that when she finished she looked at him with watery eyes. 'I have to tell you I am completely bloody mystified by the puzzle of your absent radio.'

The 11 O'Clock Moral Dilemma

Mr JPS Spagatoni leapt back. Had he heard her right? It was not her pessimism in the face of this difficult case that horrified him, although that did as well; it was her use of the B word.

'Mma!' he cried. 'What is wrong with you?'

CHAPTER FIVE

Mma Ontoaste has a drunken realisation but is bitten by a snake on the ankle and then falls in the pumpkin patch (again).

If lunch at the Salt 'N' Sauce Scotch Chip Supper Shop had not gone according to plan, thought Mma Ontoaste, it was not her doing. As she had learned over the years, it was always easier to advise other people how to live their lives. The difficulty came, thought Mma Ontoaste, as she found the bottle of neat spirit and a dusty glass on the top shelf in her grass hut, with one's own life. It was never so easy to know what one ought to do oneself. Today though, she felt like getting absolutely shit-faced, so she thought that is what she ought to do.

And it was later that evening, just as Mma Ontoaste was stumbling towards the vegetable patch to find a pumpkin to soak up the booze, that it happened. It struck her as she was crossing the yard to her grass hut. She realised suddenly that she had changed. She was no longer the Mma Ontoaste of old. She was no longer full of the kindly wisdom, the love of her land, with the insight and the strength to endure Africa's countless hardships.

As she stood rooted in the middle of her shabby yard, looking at her unkempt grass hut, she found herself wondering why she could not have just forgiven Mma Pollosopresso for being so stupid as to only get 97 per cent in her final examination at the Napier Secretarial College. Was not forgiveness what Mma Ontoaste was all about? And if that was so, then why could she not have forgiven that Nigerian for working for the Botswana Postal Service? She had not even bothered to think for a single minute about the circumstances that might make a man, even a Nigerian, eke out an honest living delivering mail when he should be 'phishing' for the details of old ladies' bank accounts. Why had she developed this sudden taste for Irn-Bru? And why was she now riding around Gaborone on a cow?

But there was more to it than that. Why had she been unable to find out who it really was who had blown up her tiny white van? Why had she just blamed Mma Pollosopresso? And why was she unable to tell that good man, Mr JPS Spagatoni, where his radio had gone? And what about the woman whose husband had gone to work on the bus? That sort of problem should have been meat and drink to a detective of Mma Ontoaste's stature.

It struck Mma Ontoaste forcibly then that she had lost her powers of detection but, worse than that, worse than almost anything, she had lost the delightful Feel Good Factor. She was no longer the Miss Read for the 21st century and Gaborone was no longer the sub-Saharan Fairacre that it had once been.

Mma Ontoaste stood in the yard staring up at the huge white moon that had risen overhead. She started to weep and she let the bitter tears roll down her cheeks and hang off her chin.

'Oh Rra!' she cried aloud. 'Oh, Rra!'

And it was then that the snake bit her.

There are more than 60 types of snake in Botswana, but of these only 12 are venomous, so although Mma Ontoaste was unlucky to be bitten by one of these 12 poisonous snakes, a snake known as the lebolobolo, she was at least lucky that it was a baby lebolobolo.

It was not, however, the relative youth of the snake that had saved the life of Mma Ontoaste. Rather it was the fact that less than quarter of an hour after the snake had bitten her, the stock gate had been pushed open and a woman carrying the most enormous elephant gun you have ever seen had entered the yard and pointed the muzzle at the head of her very nearly late ex-employer.

CHAPTER SIX

Mma Pollosopresso saves the day but Mr JPS Spagatoni is carted off to hospital where he may or may not die.

Mma Pollosopresso had always been frightened of snakes and she guessed immediately what had happened to her ex-employer. But as she stood there, pointing the huge gun at Mma Ontoaste's temple, it occurred to her that this might have made a very fine 11 o'clock Moral Dilemma. If Mma Pollosopresso did not shoot her, then Mma Ontoaste would certainly die from the snakebite, wouldn't she? So she was, in effect, already dead, which meant that if Mma Pollosopresso shot her now, would she really be killing her? Would she not just be shooting a dead body? Even the law might be vague on that one. Mma Pollosopresso realised with a slight chuckle that the only person who might be able to hand down some sort of opinion on this matter might be the very person who was about to die: Mma Ontoaste.

It would be interesting to hear her opinion. And now that she, Mma Pollosopresso, had set up her own Detective Agency, <u>The Only Detective Agency You Will Ever Need Ever! No. 4</u>, they could debate the matter as equals, detective to detective. Oh that would be fun.

Mma Pollosopresso took her finger off the trigger and put the gun aside. She bent down and placed a careful hand on the detective's neck. A ragged pulse was still beating. Mma Pollosopresso knew that she had to act fast: water and antivenom were vital, as well as some kind of pressure immobilisation that would prevent the venom leaking into Mma Ontoaste's lymphatic system. But first Mma Pollosopresso would have to find the bite to know where she could apply her tourniquet.

It was as Mma Pollosopresso was searching the body of the redoubtable founder of <u>The Best Detective Agency in the World Ever! No. 2</u> for snakebites that Mr JPS Spagatoni, that good man, returned from his day at the Salt-'n'-Sauce Scotch Chip Supper Shop on Murieston Road, out by the old UDF headquarters. As usual, it had been a long day for Mr JPS Spagatoni. He had started drinking his first 80/- beer of the day at about four that afternoon, a little while after Mma Ontoaste's disastrous visit, and so he was now quite tanked. He was being half supported, half carried by one of the trainees, Dennis, and Mr JPS Spagatoni's accent, always stronger when he had been drinking, made the song he was singing as they weaved their way up the road under the sodium glare of the street lights difficult to understand. Under one arm he was carrying four tins of 80/- beer and a half bottle of blended malt whisky and so it did not look as if he planned to end the day with an early night.

When they reached the yard, Dennis led his boss across to the toilet, an outside hut the practicalities of which no one ever really went into. While Mr JPS Spagatoni was micturating noisily into the bucket, Dennis noticed Mma Pollosopresso and Mma Ontoaste in the pumpkin patch.

'Mma, what are you doing?' he asked.

'Oh Dennis,' replied Mma Pollosopresso. 'Mma Ontoaste has

been bitten by a snake. Will you run to the hospital in Bobonong to get some antivenom and to ask them to send a bus to collect her and take her there?'

Dennis understood the urgency and, once he had put Mr JPS Spagatoni in that good man's favourite chair on the veranda, he set off for the hospital almost at once. It was only when Mr JPS Spagatoni was on the other side of two of the cans of 80/- and half of the whisky that he looked up and noticed Mma Pollosopresso in the garden. He had been keeping up a steady soliloquy on the evils of people from South Africa, Zimbabwe, Zambia, Namibia, Angola, Mozambique, Malawi and, of course, the Democratic Republic of Congo all the while, and as she searched Mma Ontoaste's body, Mma Pollosopresso knew that it was only a short matter of time before Mr JPS Spagatoni would begin to mourn the death of Bonnie Prince Charlie with tears coursing down his stubbly cheeks. After that he would ordinarily start throwing bottles and cursing the English before collapsing in a puddle of his own making.

But now he frowned into the darkness of the Botswana night and tried to work out what was going on. At first he thought it was an optical illusion. Then he thought his wife was being robbed. This stirred him to action. He staggered to his feet and made to rush at Mma Pollosopresso, waving his bottle of whisky like a *knobkerrie*.

'Ah'll 'ave ya! Ah'll . . . Aaaah!'

Mr JPS Spagatoni, that drunk man, tripped on the stoop and fell heavily, the bottle of whisky spinning out of his hand and rattling across the setts to vanish under some unnamed bush. Mma Pollosopresso stood for a moment and watched nervously as he tried to right himself. He burped deeply and then vomited a chunky concoction of fish and chips and whisky and beer before finally giving up the ghost and subsiding with a muttered curse and a vague threat.

By now Mma Pollosopresso had found the bites: two tiny punctures on Mma Ontoaste's meaty calf, and then the snake itself, crushed beneath her ex-employer. Mma Pollosopresso recognised the baby lebolobolo for what it was, and compared the bulk of Mma Ontoaste with that of the snake.

The lebolobolo was not a *very* poisonous snake, was it? And a stay in the hospital in Gaborone, for all of Botswana's undoubted beauty, was not something everybody would enjoy equally. People had been known to die in the hospital, had they not? And she did not want this to happen to Mma Ontoaste. It occurred to her that, once the antivenom was administered, then perhaps it would be better if Mma Ontoaste stayed in her own bed and fought the poison where she was most comfortable.

When Dennis arrived with the minibus half an hour later, and once the antivenom was administered, Mma Pollosopresso asked the medic and the driver to help her move the redoubtable founder of The Best Detective Agency in the World Ever! No. 2 across the yard into the grass hut.

'But Mma,' began the driver. 'I have to bring a body back to the hospital. It is the rules.'

No one asked why this particular rule might be in force. It was not the time or the place. Instead the story carried on and each pair of eyes drifted down to where Mr JPS Spagatoni was lying in his pool of sick. He was much lighter than Mma Ontoaste anyway, and he looked as if he would be easier to get into the back of the minibus, and so it was decided. Once they had got him in, bumping his head on the door as they went, they moved Mma Ontoaste. It was a struggle but after half an hour they managed to drag her into her hut and onto the bed, where she lay breathing heavily but regularly.

And all that Mma Pollosopresso and Dennis needed to do was sit there and watch, occasionally pouring sips of water into her mouth and now and then mopping her brow with one of the countless pieces of lint that that not-so-good man Mr JPS Spagatoni kept lying about the place. All through the night, as the antivenom took hold, Mma Pollosopresso kept up her bedside vigil as her ex-employer hovered between life and death. It was an uncomfortable night for all concerned, but by dawn ('sudden' and 'tropical') it began to look as if the redoubtable founder of <u>The Best Detective Agency in the World Ever! No. 2</u> would live, which was just as well because later that morning she was due to meet Tom Hurst, but it was more than could be said with any great certainty about Mr JPS Spagatoni, who, during the night, had received an unnecessary blood transfusion from an unqualified medic and was now lying sweating on a trolley in a corridor waiting for the attentions of a doctor who had long since gone to work in England, where the wages, if not the weather or the people, were better.

CHAPTER SEVEN

Mma Ontoaste starts early and becomes a bit confused but it is all right in the end because it did not matter very much anyway and then a trip is planned!

The sky above her was as blue as it had ever been when Mma Delicious Ontoaste found herself sitting outside the café at the Sir Seretse Kharma International Airport, staring at the mug of bush tea on the table before her. Those who knew the impressively padded founder of <u>The Best Detective Agency in the World Ever! No. 2</u>, and there were plenty of them, for Mma Ontoaste was a popular woman among the café owners and the convenience food-stall holders all around Gaborone, might have noticed that she was looking at her bush tea with some disgust. If a lady survives being bitten by a lebolobolo snake, then the last thing she wants is bush tea, she said to herself and so, with a flick of her powerful fingers, she summoned the waitress, a girl who up until that moment had been ignoring her but who now came trotting over as quickly as she could.

'Oh, Mma!' said the girl. 'I can see that you are hungry today—'

'Rum,' Mma Ontoaste said, cutting off the waitress. 'I want

some rum. A big glass. Or a bottle. Yes. A big bottle. Sharpish. And wait! A cigar. And none of the local rubbish. I want a Cuban cigar.'

And it was while she was drinking this rum, which was strong enough to make her eyes run, and smoking this cigar, that a tall young man in a pale suit emerged from the sliding doors of the main grass hut and squinted in the sunlight, obviously looking for someone. In each hand he held a suitcase: one of the suitcases was of ordinary proportions while the other suitcase was long and thin, as if it might have held a snooker cue, or a fly-fishing rod, and these were both possibilities the man had allowed to customs officials on his way from London Heathrow.

The Englishman was very pasty-skinned, with a mop of straight hair, thin lips and the most eerie blue eyes that Mma Ontoaste could imagine. He stood for a second, trying to get his bearings, looking perhaps for the taxi queue, until he fumbled for some sunglasses and slid them up his pointed nose. That was better, thought Mma Ontoaste, and she waved an arm in the air to attract his attention.

Tom Hurst had never been to Africa before and would have had no idea what to expect had the Dean not insisted he take a copy of *When the Lion Feeds* by Wilbur Smith with him to read on the flight. Tom now saw the fat woman waving at him and he knew from the pictures that had lined the walls of the refectory at Cuff College that this must be Mma Ontoaste herself.

'I see you, Nkosikazi!' he said, removing his bush hat and placing it on the table so that Mma Ontoaste could admire the leopard-skin hatband.

When a man comes to Africa for the first time in his life, he is usually taken by the happiness he finds all around him. People have the time to stand and stare on that continent, and they avail themselves of it, fulsomely, as is right and proper. What, after all, is life if we do not have the time to stand around the place and just watch others? Of course, there are some countries where peace and happiness do not reign universally or continually, as even Mr JPS Spagatoni, that proud African, might go so far as to admit, but Botswana was not one of those countries. Of course it had its fair share of problems, what country did not? But it was still the best country in the world and, although she was by now quite drunk, Mma Ontoaste was still the best woman in that country and now, as the rum and the antivenom mixed in her bloodstream, she began to realise that, because she was the best woman in the best country in the world, that surely meant that she was the best woman in the world and anyone who disagreed with her would get what was coming to them, white man or not, and no mistake.

'Hello, Rra,' Mma Ontoaste said, blowing a series of aggressive smoke rings into the warm Botswana air. Tom Hurst sat down at the table opposite Mma Ontoaste. After a minute the waitress brought him his bush tea and then she stood there for a second giggling behind her hand while he took a sip. She had obviously never seen a white man drinking bush tea before. Or perhaps she had never seen a white man wearing a full safari suit, complete with epaulettes and patch pockets. Or perhaps it was the other present that Wikipedia had forced on Mr T Hurst as he waited for his flight: a *sjambok* (also known, Wikipedia explained, as an *imvubu* – Zulu for hippopotamus – or a *kiboko* – the same animal in Kiswahili – or *mnigolo* in Malinké, and there was quite a lot of other information besides).

The Dean and Wikipedia had led Tom to expect a large, thoughtful woman given to philosophical pronouncements of happy banality, but here was a terse, drawn, distracted woman, drinking rum and smoking a cigar and it not yet midday.

'It's very kind of you to agree to help me, Ms Ontoaste,' Tom started. Mma Ontoaste grunted and exhaled another pile of smoke rings.

'The Dean and Professor Wikipedia send their regards,' he tried again, but this time Mma Ontoaste just shrugged carelessly. This was going to be harder work than he thought.

'I will get right to it, then, if you don't mind. The Dean tells me that you might be able to help me with this.'

He pulled from the long thin case something Mma Ontoaste only vaguely recognised as a spear.

'A spear,' she said.

'Yes,' Tom said with a smile. 'Do you recognise it?'

Mma Ontoaste thought for a minute. Why should she recognise it?

'It's not mine,' she said after a pause. 'You think that because I am an African I know about spears?'

'No—'

'And witchcraft? And cannibalism? How to bribe officials? How to *take* a bribe? How to strip and reassemble an AK47 in the dark? Just because I am an African?'

Tom was startled.

'It comes from Botswana,' he said.

'Tch! Botswana. I go on about it enough, with all this the sun blazing down, but today it seems just like a foul and pestilent congregation of vapours.'

'Right,' Tom said, sitting back. 'I can see you are not in the mood for this.'

'No,' she said, looking away, a tear in her eye. 'I am not in the mood for this.'

Tom recalled the Dean telling him that the College's detectives had not been as effective as usual, that they had been getting things wrong and hitting too many dead ends. This was the first time he had come across someone so depressed that they had given up altogether.

'You are obviously a bit depressed, Ms Ontoaste,' he said. 'I know that ordinarily that is good in a detective, but—'

Mma Ontoaste held up a large hand to stop him.

'I know, Rra. I know. It is what sets me apart. But ever since my tiny white van was destroyed I have been having doubts.'

'Doubts?'

'Yes. Doubts. Well, maybe not doubts.'

'I see. And who destroyed your van, Ms Ontoaste?' the white man asked.

'I do not know, Rra,' said Mma Ontoaste. 'I do not know.'

It suddenly occurred to her that she had not really bothered to find out what happened to her van. That was where it had all started to go wrong. Again fat tears rolled down her cheeks. This was awful. Mma Ontoaste was reduced to drinking rum and weeping at eleven in the morning. Tom would have to do something about it. Perhaps she needed a break? A change of scene? But first he would have to find out why someone had used this spear to stab Claire Morgan in the Library back at Cuff College.

It was just as Tom Hurst was returning the spear to its case that he became aware of an elderly, scholarly-looking man at the next table. He had a round face and a fuzz of grey hair and was peering at them over the top of his gold-framed *pince-nez*. He was wearing a 15-piece tropical-weight tartan suit and had been sitting with a book on medical ethics and a copy of *African Adventure* by a man called Willard Price, which was a book that Tom had read as a boy and gleaned enough information from it about the various predators of the Savannah to win some sort of science prize and therefore give hope to his father and his father's father that he might have some future in the Genre.

The old gent at the next-door table was drinking tea from a cup and saucer and occasionally jotting down little observations and *pensées* in a commonplace book by his side. He appeared to be wearing heavy dark make-up – as if for one of those shows where white men played black men, or *Othello* – and behind it his bright blue eyes twinkled like those of a mischievous schoolboy.

'I say,' he said politely in a rather smart accent. 'I do hope you'll excuse an interruption from an old chap like me, but I wonder if that is not a rather rare and valuable assegai? It looks just like the one in the collection of the Botswana National Museum.'

Mma Ontoaste rolled her eyes.

'That's all we need,' she groaned. This sort of thing happened to her all the time these days; some clever bloody dick who knew what he was talking about. What about feminine intuition? What about sympathy and human bloody understanding?

The man introduced himself as Sandi Rudisandi, a Lecturer in Medical Ethics at the University of Gaborone and from there it was only a matter of time until, with Sandi Rudisandi's help, Mma Ontoaste and Tom made their way to the National Museum of Botswana and the Curator's office in a small well-kept grass hut, separated from the main grass hut by a concrete path.

'Would you like some bush tea, Mma?' he began, settling himself down behind his desk for a long talk in the old-fashioned Botswana fashion.

'Oh, God save us, Rra,' cried Mma Ontoaste, a heavy fist thumping sloppily on the desk. 'Don't you have anything stronger?'

'Perhaps we ought to get to the matter of the spear?' Tom suggested. He cast a worried eye towards Mma Ontoaste. She was beginning to look rather bedraggled and unfocused. Sandi Rudisandi was blinking owlishly and dabbing at his make-up in the heat of the grass hut.

'Oh Rra, that is a beauty,' said the Curator when Tom showed him the spear. 'Wherever did you get it?'

'Well,' Tom said. 'We were rather hoping to ask you the same question. We wondered whether we could see the one in your collection.'

The Curator paused and looked puzzled.

'Why?' he asked.

Tom looked flustered for a second. He had come all this way for – Actually, why had he come all this way? He could not really see what good it would do now. When the Dean had suggested it, it seemed absolutely the right thing to do, but now?

He recalled his training. Press on regardless. Doubt is contagious. Once a detective knows what is to come next in the plot, it is his duty to seal off all other avenues of enquiry. Better still: do not admit they might even exist.

'I believe that whoever used this assegai to kill Claire Morgan was sending us a message and that the answer lies in the National Museum of Botswana.'

There was a long silence. Tom began to feel uncomfortable with three pairs of eyes on him. None of the others looked the slightest bit convinced.

'May I see the other spear?' He changed the subject while they were still confused. 'Sandi Rudisandi says it is almost identical.'

The Curator pushed his chair back and got to his feet.

'Well, if you think it will help,' he said with a doubtful shrug. He led them down a long corridor past scale models of grass huts and broken pottery to a line of spears. They stood in front of the case and stared. There were six spears, irregularly grouped, but there were seven information labels.

'My God,' said the Curator. 'One of the spears is missing. It must have been stolen—'

It was, Tom Hurst guessed correctly, an assegai made by the *Bamangwato* tribe in what was called Bechuanaland, sometime in the 19th century.

'It must have been those gypsies from the circus,' continued the Curator. 'I thought they'd only got the life-size model of the elephant. I thought this spear had gone to be cleaned. There is a cleaning label hanging there. Look.'

The Curator pointed to a hook, halfway up the back of the glass cabinet, which had, Tom presumed, held the spear in place. From it hung a piece of string attached to a white oblong of thick paper.

'That is the sort of label the conservators use to inform people that an object has gone to be repaired or cleaned.'

Mma Ontoaste burped. Sandi Rudisandi wrinkled his nose and stepped back a pace.

'Can we see the label?' Tom asked.

'Of course,' began the Curator and he fumbled with some keys on a ring and set about opening the display case. When it was opened he stretched across to take the label and then looked at it in surprise.

'Oh!' he cried.

'What?'

'Oh, Rra! This is not good. This is not a conservation label. This looks like a price tag from a shop.'

The Curator passed the label to Tom, who turned it over, a frown puckering his brow. Although one side of the ticket was blank, the other was glossy, and a particular shade of blue that

Tom recalled seeing from his trips along the North Circular back in London. On the blue, printed in thick, upper-case yellow letters, was the word IKEA. Beneath this were printed, in a different, later, but more specific process, the words MYSA MÅNE and then a price of some sort: 179,00 kr.

Whatever did it mean? Was it another clue? He wondered if the person who had left this tag here was the same person who had removed the spear and if that spear was the same spear that had had such an unfortunate impact upon Claire Morgan. Then he thought again. Any other conclusion would render all this meaningless.

'Whoever killed Claire Morgan left this as a clue for us,' he said. 'We must find out what it means. Mr Curator, sir, have you a computer with access to the internet?'

The Curator scratched his head.

'Internet?' he said, as if he had never heard of such a thing.

'Yes. You can get onto the internet and get any amount of crazy information you want and it allows you to make the most wonderfully swooping deductive leaps. It is a basic tool of the literary detective.'

'Oh,' said the Curator. 'That. Yes. I have it in my office.'

Tom placed the spear very carefully back in the slot from which it had been taken, not for a second wondering whether it would fit or not, and the Curator locked the glass cabinet. Mma Ontoaste was fidgeting, but Sandi Rudisandi was busy taking notes as they trooped back along the path to the Curator's office.

Once they had turned on the computer the Curator brought up Google and typed the words into the search field. There was an infinitesimal pause but finally, after 0.56 seconds, a long list of hits appeared on the screen.

'A duvet?'

This was the last thing that any of them expected. MYSA MÅNE was the name of a duvet made from artificial fibres in a box construction. Whatever did it mean? Tom shook his head. A duvet? This looked like a dead end if ever there were one.

'Whoever did this is playing with us,' he said.

'I wouldn't pay 179 krona for a fucking duvet,' mumbled Mma Ontoaste. Sandi Rudisandi flinched, but Tom Hurst stopped for a second, his mouth gaping. Then he turned to her with a smile of triumph on his face.

'Ms Ontoaste! You are a genius!'

'How so?'

'Krona!'

'Krona?'

'Yes. Krona.'

And then:

'Sweden!'

'What about Sweden?'

'That's where we have to go next. To IKEA.'

Part III

The Hour of the Quilt

1

Rain

Rain.

A silent curtain of rain shutting off everything and everyone. Coming in from the Baltic. Always rain at this time of year before the winter came. Neighbour turned against neighbour, dog against cat. Could we ever truly get away from it? Could we ever truly be free? Winter would be worse though, he thought. Then there would be snow and darkness. After that the sun would shine and then there would be slush and chaos.

It was 8.30 in the morning and he was sitting in his car staring at the shuttered front of the dry-cleaner's. They were closed again. His stained suit was roughly folded into a plastic bag on the seat next to him. He did not know what he should do. Then he looked at his coffee until it grew cold.

Why had he done it?

Why had he joined the police force in the first place? Did he even want to be a police officer any more? Every day was worse than the last. Every day things got worse. Every day as a police officer he saw terrible things. The police are a microcosm of society. He wondered how long it would be before he lost his fear of being with people.

The town of Ynstead on the southernmost tip of Sweden, over-

91

looking the sea, was one of the few towns where the police actually outnumbered the population. Despite this and the lowest crime rate in Sweden, Colander would come to think of the days that followed as some of the most extraordinary in his long career as a policeman and, when he looked back upon them, he would wonder how he got through them without recourse to suicide.

He started the engine of the car. For a few moments he did not know whether to put the car in first gear or reverse. One action would mean the car went backwards, away from the grey wall in front of him, but the other action might mean the car went forward into the grey wall in front of him.

He arrived at the police station at 9.05. Toff Toffsson was on duty behind the desk in the reception area. If Toffsson was surprised to see the police officer from Ynstead, he did not show it. Colander went along the corridor to his office. He was sweating heavily. What is wrong with me now? he wondered. He removed his shirt and wiped his body with the curtains. Lemm Lemmingsson opened the door without knocking. The young policeman was surprised and embarrassed at seeing Inspector Colander naked from the waist up.

'I am sorry if I have disturbed you, Inspector,' he said. 'You called a meeting today for 8.10 and it is 8.10 already.'

Inspector Colander looked at his watch and thought for a minute. He recalled calling the meeting, but he could not remember if he had called it yesterday or a hundred years ago. I have become a stranger to time, he thought, and he could remember nothing.

Outside it was raining.

Lemmingsson stood at the door waiting.

'You had better come in,' said Colander after a while, returning his body to the shirt.

Lemmingsson sat down on one of the chairs at the table. He had a cup of coffee with him.

'Let us summarise what we know so far,' said Colander.

'To be honest, Inspector,' replied the junior police officer. 'I think we do not know very much at all.'

'I have always found that a police officer usually knows more than he thinks he does,' said Colander with a trace of annoyance.

'Perhaps you are right,' agreed Lemmingsson. He wrote something on a pad of paper with a pencil.

'We need a breakthrough,' said Colander. 'I do not think we can allow ourselves much more than a day following this line of approach.'

The two police officers agreed that they would have another meeting when they knew more and they scheduled it for eleven o'clock that evening. Just as Lemmingsson was leaving, Colander asked him something.

'See if you can get Knut Knutsson to come along,' he said. 'He may have something to add to what we have to say.'

'Yes, I will,' said Lemmingsson.

Inspector Colander collected his car from the car park and drove out of Ynstead, following the road to Malmö. On the way he stopped at a service station and ordered himself a coffee. After that he drove on, concentrating on the road and thinking only vaguely about what had happened during the morning. He was sure he had forgotten something, but could not put his finger on what it might have been.

I am empty inside, he thought, although I am also so full that I am about to burst. Why am I in such pain?

When he got to Malmö he remembered that he had not taken his suit in to the dry-cleaner's. He wondered if this was the thing that he had been trying to remember. He took a pencil and wrote the words 'dry cleaning' down on a scrap of paper that he found in his pocket.

Then he parked the car illegally across the road from the video rental shop in Malmö and waited until there was no traffic before crossing. When he opened the door a bell pinged and a man in a cardigan came from a back office.

Burt Colander introduced himself as a police officer. The owner of the video shop introduced himself as the owner of a video shop.

'Although we also stock DVDs,' he said, pointing with one hand to a long rack of DVD films. Colander turned to look at the display that the man had alerted him to, where a single man with dark hair and an old-fashioned elk-skin jacket stood with his head bowed over the selection, and then Colander looked back at the man in the cardigan.

'I will tell you why I am here,' he said.

'Good,' said the man. 'I was wondering.'

Colander explained that he was looking for a video tape. The man explained that he did not have the video tape that Colander was looking for. Colander had not expected much more than this but anyway asked him to ring the police station in Ynstead if there was anything he remembered.

'What is there to remember?' asked the man as he closed the door behind Colander and watched him cross the road to where his car was parked.

Once again Colander was struck by the thought that perhaps he was missing something. He drove back to Ynstead in the rain, trying not to think about the welcome that waited for him. When he thought of his lonely flat he thought that something had ended for him in the past. Something that he had never wanted in the first place but he was now sure had gone. He had started sweating again. He ought to go and see the doctor. But not yet. After this investigation perhaps. He took off his shirt and looked around for something with which to dry himself. Nothing, of course. He put his shirt back on.

Tord Tordsson was in charge of the one o'clock meeting. Colander informed them about his visit to the video shop in Malmö. There was a silence after he had spoken.

'Let's just be honest with ourselves,' Tordsson said. 'We do not really know anything for sure. How can we? We are just insignificant humans. We can make all the plans we like, but when something like this happens it makes you stop and wonder why.'

They all agreed with Tordsson.

'Perhaps we should divide ourselves into two groups?' Colander suggested. Everybody in the meeting room stopped and listened to him. It was if he had taken on the mantle of someone who knew what would happen next. And yet Colander had not sought out the position.

'Go on,' said Tordsson.

'Perhaps if one team concentrated on working the telephones, while the other team concentrated on door-to-door?'

'That is a good idea. Let's do that.'

They divided themselves up into teams. Colander and Lemmingsson agreed they would work together. Tordsson suggested they should have another meeting at five o'clock that afternoon to see if anyone had had a breakthrough.

'Let's keep in touch, though,' said Tordsson. 'We all know this is getting towards the most dangerous time.'

The end of the week was always bad, but Friday evenings were the worst. This was when the utter hopelessness of their existence often became intolerable and suicide became a definite option. To prevent this, the police officers kept in touch and had formed an Ingmar Bergman Film Club, which met every Friday evening to watch the Swedish master's old films.

Colander asked Lemmingsson to come to his office after the

one o'clock meeting. Before he could speak, Lemmingsson asked a question.

'What will we do if we cannot find the film we are looking for?' he asked.

'We still have until tomorrow, don't we?' replied Colander.

'Yes, but the Film Club begins at four. What if we do manage to find the film but cannot manage to get it back in time?'

'It is a problem.'

'Have you tried Helsingborg?' Lemmingsson asked.

'No,' Colander said. 'To be honest I am somewhat in the dark about Helsingborg.'

'I see.'

'In the meantime why are you always talking to me as though we were standing at the top of a hill with a strong wind blowing all around us?'

'Everyone in this area speaks like this. It is the Swedish way.'

'By the way, where is Knut Knutsson? I heard that he had arrived and yet I have not had a chance to meet this new highly-thought-of police officer from Stockholm.'

'He is in his office, I understand,' Lemmingsson said. 'Working on something.'

The telephone call came at about two o'clock in the afternoon. Toff Toffsson had been relieved on the reception desk by Son Sonsson who put the call through to Burt Colander at 2.05. At 2.06 Burt Colander picked up the telephone and spoke into the receiver.

Lemmingsson was surprised to see his boss stand up when he heard the voice on the other end of the line. Oh no, he thought, another narrative voice. Colander listened for a moment with his eyes wide in slight confusion. Lemmingsson had the impression that the call was important.

'Of course,' said Colander into the receiver. 'I will do anything I can to help.'

He wrote something on a pad of paper with his pencil. When he put the phone down, Lemmingsson thought the senior police officer looked strained and pale. He too hated it when information was rationed like this.

'Someone is coming to see me,' he said. 'Someone from abroad. An Englishman and a woman from Botswana. Where does that leave us? The world is closing in on us.'

'Yes,' agreed Lemmingsson.

Colander drank some coffee and then turned to face the wall. Will we ever truly be alone? he wondered. Or are we all destined to be tossed hither and thither until we can stand it no more. He thought of suicide often.

His coffee was cold and he could hear music coming from the office next door.

'Who has the office next door now?' he asked Lemmingsson, just as the young police officer was about to turn and walk out of the office with his by now cold cup of coffee.

'That is Knut Knutsson,' said Lemmingsson. 'He has brought a radio with him.'

'I do not like music generally,' said Colander.

'Nor me,' agreed Lemmingsson.

'But this is nice. It has a nice rhythm. It seems as if the person playing the instrument knows how to play a tune.'

'He might not be Swedish,' cautioned Lemmingsson.

Lemmingsson gathered his coffee cup and said goodbye to Colander. Inspector Colander followed him down the corridor but, instead of turning left at the end, as Lemmingsson had, the inspector turned right and out into the car park.

He got into his car and drove home. He was just about to

park outside his flat when he remembered his dry-cleaning. He drove to the dry-cleaner's and gave them the suit, remembering to point out that there was a stain on the lapel from when he had spilled some pizza. When he got back into the car, despite the distant rumble of mental thunder to remind him there was still the problem of the foreigners who were coming to see him, Colander felt he had achieved something. He tapped his fingers on the steering wheel as he drove, recalling the music he had heard through Knut Knutsson's wall.

He intended, as usual, to lie down when he got to his flat, but instead he felt unnaturally energised. All the while that tune from Knut Knutsson's office ran through his mind as he found a roll of black bin bags and swept all the pizza cartons from the kitchen table into one of them. Next he changed the sheets on his bed. Then he flushed all the whisky and vodka down the lavatory pan and then all the pills and the coffee. There was almost nothing left in the flat now. He took down one of the five oil paintings from the wall. He removed the simple wooden frame and broke it into pieces over his knee. He pushed the pieces in the wood-burning stove and then set them alight with a match that lit first time. He studied the picture at arm's length. A picture of a parrot in a wooden sauna. It had to go. It was a shame that they were his father's paintings, but never mind. He folded it up and forced it into the flames. When the fire took hold the oil paint burned with an acrid black smoke that poured out of the wood-burner. Soon the overhead sprinklers activated and a fine rain soaked everything that was left in the house.

Such things happen in a sophisticated modern society, thought Inspector Colander. I should be glad that the smoke did not asphyxiate me, nor the building set itself on fire. Besides, the water was refreshing. He undressed and stood for a while in the sitting room, enjoying the feel of it falling on his back and also the mossy feel of the carpet between his toes. Then he rubbed his clothes with soap from the bathroom. Soon they were clean enough to put back on.

All in all, a good day.

It was too far to drive to Helsingborg that evening and he had a meeting with Lemm Lemmingsson scheduled for later, so Inspector Colander decided to run to the police station. He felt the need for some exercise. Maybe he should lose a little weight, he thought. He dug out an old tracksuit and a pair of trainers and set off at a decent pace.

He could have gone straight to the police station but instead diverted past the video shop in Hamngatan. It was from here that the police officers usually got their videos for the Ingmar Bergman Film Club and as such it was at the heart of this investigation. Yellow and blue police tape sealed off the door and a junior police officer was standing guarding the entrance.

He greeted Inspector Colander and removed some of the tape to let his superior into the shop.

Inside it was just as Colander remembered it. Nothing seemed to have changed. The man behind the counter was looking somewhat bored. Since the police had closed the shop he had had no customers. He looked at the inspector aggressively.

'What do you want?'

'Information,' snapped Colander. He was in no mood to talk. 'Has the video been returned?'

'How can it have been returned when you have closed my shop? No one can get in or out.'

'Don't play games with me. Tell me who took it out and when.'

'I keep telling you, my records are confidential.'

'And I keep telling you that I am a policeman and I need to know everything.'

The two men stared at one another. Neither looked like yielding until the man behind the counter sighed.

'I can't very well make a living like this,' he said. 'All right. I will show you my files.'

Was this the breakthrough Colander had been looking for, he wondered. I have waited so long, he thought, but I must not expect too much. After all, what will this man's records reveal that I do not already suspect?

The man sat behind a monitor and began typing in the words necessary.

'The film is due back on Saturday,' he said after a moment.

'Saturday? Saturday is too late. I need it tomorrow.'

'Well,' shrugged the man. 'You cannot have it unless he brings it back early and since the shop is shut, I do not expect him to do that, do you?'

Colander thought for a minute. He would have to take the man off the door.

'All right,' he said. 'You can open the shop again, but I am going to have to have a name.'

There was a long pause. Finally the man behind the terminal read out a name and an address.

'Knut Knutsson, Hamngatan 219, Ynstead. Just along the road.'

Knut Knutsson. The name of the highly-thought-of police officer from Stockholm. Could they be one and the same? And, if so, what was Knut Knutsson doing with the video tape? This was something for which Colander had not prepared himself. Knut Knutsson had only just arrived from Stockholm and already he had joined the video shop and taken out the very film the Film Club wanted. Colander left the man in the video shop and told the man on the door to clean up and get back to the station.

Toff Toffsson was back behind the desk in reception. He had with him a cup of coffee.

'Good afternoon, Inspector,' he said. 'I see you are in a track-suit.'

'Yes, that's right, Toff. A tracksuit.'

Toffsson looked up sharply. Toffsson had had no idea that Colander knew his given name. More alarming was the fact that ordinarily Colander only donned his tracksuit and trainers toward the end of his cases, when it was time for him to act out of character and blunder about the woods in the dark. As far as anyone had informed the receptionist, the case had not progressed that far yet.

Colander knocked on the door of Knut Knutsson's office. Although that music was still playing, there was no answer. He tried the door handle. It was locked.

Colander's meeting with Tord Tordsson started. Tordsson ran the meeting and he began by outlining the situation so far.

'Although we do not know anything for sure,' he said, 'we need a breakthrough. But we should bear in mind that, even if we do find a link between what we know and what we don't know, there is no guaranteeing it will lead us to what we want to know.'

'I do not know why we bother,' said Colander quietly. He could hear that delightful music coming from Knut Knutsson's office.

'Perhaps you would like to tell us about the film you have chosen for the Ingmar Bergman Film Club, Inspector,' rebuked Tordsson.

Colander explained what had happened at the video shop in Hamngatan.

'Has anyone actually laid eyes on the highly regarded police officer from Stockholm?'

There was a general shaking of heads.

'You mean the nationally known one? No. I have not seen him. It is somewhat mysterious.'

Silence followed, so that Colander thought he might as well mention the two foreigners who were coming to see him.

'They are coming to Ynstead?'

'Yes.'

'They cannot join our Ingmar Bergman Film Club.'

'No.'

The meeting broke up when Lemmingsson entered the room with a cup of coffee to start his meeting with Colander and Tordsson. Tordsson recapped on the earlier meeting and then Lemmingsson took over and ran the meeting.

'Perhaps the two foreigners might be allowed to join the Ingmar Bergman Film Club if we are not watching an Ingmar Bergman film?' he suggested.

'That is one idea,' said Tordsson dismissively. Why should foreigners appreciate Bergman?

'We do not know if the foreigners will even be in time for the screening of the film anyway, so all this might be academic,' said Nog Noggsson, who had come in to join the meeting.

'We should find out when they are arriving.'

Lemm Lemmingsson agreed that he would ring the airline company in Stockholm.

'Are there enough chairs in the television room?'

Again Lemmingsson agreed to check. He is shouldering the lion's share of the investigation, thought Colander. Tordsson suggested they ask Knut Knutsson to come to the screening.

'It might smoke him out,' he said.

'And he can bring his own chair if it is an issue.'

Again Lemmingsson agreed to count the chairs.

'Do you know why the foreigners are coming to our shores, Inspector Colander?'

Inspector Colander was doodling love hearts in a pad of paper with a pencil and was thinking about something else. The meeting broke up. The police officers went their separate ways. Colander drove to see his father. Why am I so cheerful? he wondered. He had felt elated all day. It was true that he could not concentrate for a second, but still. What, he wondered, would the next day bring?

Later Colander would recall the next few hours as among the most ordinary he had ever spent as a police officer. He drove along the E13 towards Sjöbo, to where his father lived. There was too much left to chance. He felt as if he were shooting off in the wrong direction and yet there was something that Lemmingsson had said, or perhaps had left out, that made Colander think. He rang the police officer on the car telephone. Lemmingsson picked up the phone on the third ring.

'Why are you ringing me?' he asked.

'There was something you said in the meeting. Or something you did not say in the meeting. It makes me think we are on to something.'

'I can show you my notes of that meeting at the meeting this afternoon.'

'I thought the meeting was scheduled for this evening?'

'We are having another meeting first at the police station to go over the case so far at four o'clock. I can bring my notes then.'

'I am sure it is nothing.'

Colander put down the phone.

His father had married a Thai bride almost exactly 30 years Inspector Colander's junior. To begin with, their relationship had been strained. What was a Thai woman doing in Sweden? Inspector

103

Colander had tried to have her deported. The wedding ceremony was rushed but nonetheless official, even if the garbled vows to love one another 'long time' were not completely by the book.

When he arrived at his father's house it was almost seven o'clock in the evening and it had been dark for eight hours. His step-mother greeted him at the door with a rice dish and a slight bow. His father was in the sauna, she said, painting the parrot. When she had first said this, Colander had thought it was a euphemism for something far darker, but that in fact was what his father was doing.

Inspector Colander's father only ever painted interiors of his sauna, but they were so lavishly detailed that one could see the grain of wood of each plank and in this way they differed subtly. Another difference was that in some there was a parrot while in others there was none. To be completely honest, Burt Colander did not know the significance of the parrot. He was not completely sure his father did either.

'I will not disturb him,' said Colander.

'Okay,' said the woman from MyThaiBride.org.

'Is he all right? I worry about him.'

'Yeh yeh,' she said. 'Same same but different.'

Colander drove home. We are not always alone, he thought, for the first time in many years. It is possible to find consolation. It might be with a parrot. Or it might be with an Ingmar Bergman double bill. Or it might be with a young Thai girl.

Before he drove home, Colander removed the scatter cushions on the back seat of the car and dabbed at his armpits. Then he returned the cushions to the car and set off. As he drove, he had an idea. It was a desperate gamble, but it might just work. He picked the phone up again and rang Tord Torddsson. Tord Tordsson could not believe what the inspector asked him to do but, once Colander explained his plan, he agreed to do it nonetheless.

The press conference was called for eight o'clock that evening – in time for the late editions – and it was to be held in the conference room. It may be too late, thought Colander, but it was worth one last desperate try. He spent the next hour rehearsing his answers, trying to imagine every conceivable question. The journalists – a man from the *Ynstead Examiner* and another from the *Sjöbo Chronicle* – sat and took notes in their pads of paper as Inspector Colander explained the developments in the case so far. When he had finished, there was silence for a while, except for a reedy buzzing snore from the nose of the man from the *Sjöbo Chronicle*.

He had time for only one question afterwards and it came from the man from the *Ynstead Examiner*.

'Yes,' said Colander, pointing at the man with his hand up. 'You.'

'So you cannot find a copy of *The Hour of the Wolf* on video and you would like any member of the public who might be able to help to get in touch with the Ynstead police station? Is that right?'

'Yes,' agreed Colander. From the back of the room Tordsson gave him a nod of approval. It was a desperate gamble, but time was very tight. If they could not find the film, what then?

Colander called the press conference to a close.

'Okay, that's it. A full lid.'

After the press conference Colander collected his car and then went home. He slept soundly that night and was only woken by the telephone trilling damply from the sitting room.

'Hello,' he said, standing naked by the window. Even in the cold air he could tell that his problems with erectile dysfunction seemed to be clearing themselves up of their own accord.

The voice on the other end said something in English. Inspector Colander listened and then agreed that he would drive to the airport in Stockholm to collect the two foreigners. He had to be back in time for the Film Club. He thought perhaps that he had been premature in his thoughts about his erectile dysfunction.

The meeting began promptly at ten and, as soon as he saw the faces gathered around the table, Colander knew that the breakthrough they had all been hoping for had not occurred. No one had found a copy of the film. They had only a very few hours before they were due to show it and Colander was still trying to think desperately of a way in which he might discover a copy.

He picked up Lemm Lemmingsson on the way to the airport and, as they drove towards Stockholm on the E22, Lemmingson asked Inspector Colander about the two foreigners whom they were going to collect. Colander saw that Lemmingsson had brought a gun with him.

'The man from England is from my old College,' he explained. 'He is a Lecturer in Transgression and Pathology.'

'Why is he coming to Sweden? Why is he coming here to Ynstead?'

'He is here because he wants to buy a duvet.'

'A duvet?'

'Yes.'

'Oh.'

A silence followed. Inspector Colander concentrated on the road. They passed the turn-offs to Kristianstad and Karlskrona and then Västervik before Lemmingsson spoke again.

'And what about the other foreigner?'

'The other foreigner is a private detective from Botswana.'

'Botswana?'

'Yes.'

'Oh. What does he want?'

'Also to buy a duvet.'

The car reached the turn-offs for Norrköping and then Nyköping before Lemmingsson asked if there was much call for duvets in Botswana.

'To tell you the truth,' said Colander. 'I am as much in the dark about Botswana as you are.'

'Perhaps we can ask him when we see him?'

'That is a good idea,' agreed Colander. Lemmigsson was coming along as a police officer, he thought.

At the airport, the policemen went through security channels and met the two foreigners straight from the jet. They were easy to spot. The man was wearing a beige safari suit and a hunting hat while the other, who transpired to be a woman, and who was extremely large and black, was wearing a dress made from a vast amount of gaudy red material that looked as if it might have been bought at a street market. They had obviously not had time to pack properly.

The police officer from Ynstead identified himself to the foreigners.

Inspector Colander recalled Delicious Ontoaste instantly. It had been long ago, some time in a past with which he was by now only distantly familiar, but she had been such a well-thought-of character that she was not easily forgotten. She seemed to remember him as well.

'Oh Rra! I know you! You were at Cuff College in Oxford, weren't you? What is your name again? Fred Sieve? Something like that.'

The detective from Ynstead introduced himself afresh. He was startled by the abundance of the woman. While at College he had spent many hours in a small café drinking tea and feeling home sick, but he had always been aware of the thin black girl who had spent most of her time weeping in the bathroom and who would buttonhole people to talk about her father and a man called Sir Seretse Kharma, of whom no one had ever heard. Colander recalled that she had failed many of her exams, but had surprised them all with a paper that circumvented the Holmesian Dictum. Colander could remember that her theory was not that the elimination of the impossible led to the discovery of the solution, however impossible that might seem, but that if a man looked bad, he probably was. It had been startling in its simplicity and had scored a pass.

And now here she was, standing in Stockholm Airport, larger than life, smelling of cocoa butter and carrying an airline blanket under her arm. Already the customs officers were buzzing towards her.

Tom Hurst, meanwhile, looked thunderstruck. He kept looking between one and the other. He had not known that they were acquainted with one another.

Introductions were made. Lemmingsson kept a continuous smile on his face. Being from Ynstead, he had never seen a black lady before, let alone met one, let alone touched one. He smelled his hand after he had shaken hers. It smelled pleasant.

Inspector Colander checked his watch. They were running late. Leaving Lemmingsson to stare at Mma Ontoaste, he took the man from England aside.

'We have to get back to Ynstead in time for the Ingmar Bergman Film Club meeting at four o'clock. In the meantime I have to check the headlines of the *Ynstead Exami*ner and the *Sjöbo Chronicle*.'

'But we need to get to an IKEA before they close,' Tom Hurst said.

'It will have to wait until tomorrow, I am afraid. This is an emergency.'

Tom Hurst nodded.

'All right,' he said. 'But listen. You have to tell me how you know Mma Ontoaste.'

'We were at College together. Didn't the Dean tell you? The Class of '74. Terry Jacks's song "Seasons in the Sun" was number one in the United Kingdom.'

'I see,' mumbled Tom, deep in thought, stepping back as Colander found a copy of the *Ynstead Examiner* and began translating the headline for him. A herring had been found by a child out walking his dog by the harbour. The fish showed signs of horrific violence to its person – its guts had been removed and its body cavity cleaned completely – so that the paper was calling for a police investigation.

Inspector Colander swore. Not only would that take up more police time – and they were working flat out now – but it also meant that the story of the missing video and the police appeal for information as to its whereabouts only made it to page five.

The *Sjöbo Chronicle* led with a story about the ongoing campaign to have the limb of a pine tree that had grown over a public right of way removed. It was seen as a health hazard and yet the council had done nothing about it for almost two days now.

Colander had to accept that his latest efforts had been in vain.

All four of them piled into the car; Colander drove with Mma Ontoaste in the front seat next to him. She was slightly taken aback by the ordinary choice of car until Colander explained that he normally drove a sledge pulled by reindeer but that the snows[6]

---

6 Hoohoo! Another mention of meteorological conditions. I wonder what this
   one is supposed to mean.

had failed them this year. At that Mma Ontoaste was impressed.

Tom Hurst and Lemm Lemmingsson sat in the back. Hurst was relieved. On the flight to London and then on to Stockholm, he had had to sit in economy next to Mma Ontoaste. The African lady had overflowed her own seat and bulged into his, so that, by the end of the flight, he had lost all feeling in his left side.

As they drove back down the E22, Lemmingsson then mentioned to his superior that he had, as suggested, brought his notes from the meeting the day before, as he had been asked to do. Colander was surprised. Normally this sort of detail was left hanging.

'There was something Lemmingsson said or did not say at a meeting the other day that made me think of something,' explained Colander.

As Lemmingsson read his notes through, repeating the details of the case so far, both the foreigners began to grasp the complexity of the investigation.

'There!' said Tom Hurst in the back, just as Lemmingsson got to the bit after Tord Tordsson had told the meeting that the foreigners would not be allowed to watch the Ingmar Bergman film and Lemmingsson suggested that they ought to be allowed to watch if the film were not an Ingmar Bergman film.

'If you don't watch an Ingmar Bergman film, then we can watch with you, can't we? And, since you don't have an Ingmar Berman film to watch, we might just as well get another film. Then we could watch that with you.'

Colander glanced at Mma Ontoaste. She was a beautiful woman he thought, with dark shiny skin and eyes that seemed to twinkle brownly.

'Hang on, Lemmingsson,' said Colander. 'Please go back a second and read that bit again.'

Lemmingsson started again. When he had repeated the exchange, Colander held his hand up.

'We could get another video and show that instead of the Ingmar Bergman film,' he said. 'Then Mma Ontoaste and the detective from England could join us.'

There was a slight pause before the others in the car agreed with him. By the time they reached Ynstead, it had stopped raining and the rest of the passengers were in agreement with Inspector Colander and his plan. One or two details needed clearing up but it was about now that Colander began thinking ahead. How could he somehow claim that it was all a team effort and that he had nothing to do with the solution while also making sure that everybody knew he had been the key? He had managed it in all his other cases, but this one looked as if it might be trickier.

Meanwhile his eye kept meeting that of Mma Ontoaste. She was certainly not quite as he recalled her from his days at College, but she was nevertheless an attractive woman and, despite her clothes, he could see that she was very shapely.

'I am wondering, too, Rra, if there is not somewhere we can go to buy some different clothes. We left in such a hurry, you see? And I am just wearing this old thing.'

Colander glanced at the dress Mma Ontoaste was holding between her sizeable fingers. She had pulled it up to show him and accidentally she had exposed her knees. They were fine and brown and round with no trace of the pale skin that came from kneeling and washing floors.

Colander thought for a minute. It was true. Neither of the two foreigners could realistically be expected to discover anything dressed in the manner in which they were. He glanced at his watch again.

'There is an outfitters in Ynstead,' suggested Lemmingsson. 'In

111

Hamngatan. Next to the video shop. We can go there and still be in time for the Film Club.'

As Colander parked the blue Peugeot the sun came out.

'Oh Rra, this is very pretty,' said Mma Ontoaste, looking about at the views along the cobbled street down to the enclosed harbour and the sliver of golden sand.

'Cobbled streets and well-tended houses. Everybody so considerate and kind.'

Colander did not see it like that, of course. For every cobbled street lined with neat whitewashed cottages that Mma Ontaoste saw, Colander saw a dismal alley separating opium dens, child brothels and illegal S & M dungeons, but he said nothing. Instead he led them across the cobbled street to the outfitters. He entrusted Lemmingsson with the trip to the video shop.

'You know what to do?'

Lemmingsson nodded.

'And do not forget to keep in touch. I will be on my mobile. I want you to ring every two minutes with an update. I will show Mma Ontoaste and this Lecturer from England what to buy and then I will come over to help.'

Again Lemmingsson nodded.

'Good luck.'

Lemmingsson walked quickly up the street, keeping to the shadows, making certain no one followed him, to where the video shop was by now open again. They had their plan worked out and, barring any unforeseen events, they hoped that, if they stuck to it, it would transpire to be a success.

Colander, Mma Ontoaste and Tom Hurst entered the shop. It was a traditional outfitter and five minutes later they emerged dressed in traditional Swedish clothes. Mma Ontoaste wore a classic reindeer leather cap from Bulan and an elegant reindeer waistcoat over her Skjaeveland sweater (strictly Norwegian, but she did not seem to mind very much) of red and blue and white above a long purple velvet skirt. On her feet she had a pair of Båstad clogs, which clonked nosily on the cobbles. It is hard to convey how stupid she looks, thought Colander, but there was something about her.

'Oh Rra, I will never get used to these.'

Tom Hurst wore a summer cap of similar reindeer leather and the same sort of waistcoat and jumper, but a pair of thick worsted fisherman's trousers and on his feet a pair of blacksmith's clogs from Skånetoffeln. It surprised even Colander how quickly they blended in with the other 16,000 people who lived in Ynstead.

Meanwhile Lemmingsson had returned from the video shop with a video of *Braveheart*, a film made in 1995, directed by and starring Mel Gibson.

'Should it not be Mel Gibsson?' asked Lemmingsson when he read the credits.

'He does not look very Swedish, though,' said Colander. 'But then he does not look very Scotch either, which is what he is supposed to be.'

There was a long pause.

'In this film at least.'

Another long pause.

'It was the only film left in the shop,' he explained with a shrug of his shoulders.

Colander glanced at his watch. It was half past four already and the Film Club was due to begin at five o'clock. Ordinarily, it would be time for some hair-raising driving, but the police station was only round the corner so a sedate walk would see them taking their seats at the correct time.

As they walked up towards the police station, Colander began to grasp that the investigation was over. He had failed to find a copy of *The Hour of the Wolf*. He had failed to have a high-speed car chase. He had failed to wallow around in his tracksuit in the dark with a gun he did not know how to use. He had failed to have everyone in the police station work harder than they knew they could.

So why did he feel so happy?

Was it because he was walking next to Mma Ontoaste, the most striking woman with the most singular intelligence he had met since that strange Latvian woman whom none of his readers really believed existed? She had sounded like the sort of thing a boarding-school boy, unfamiliar with women, might make up, now that he thought about it.

The impact the two foreigners made on the Ingmar Bergman Film Club is hard to exaggerate and, when Colander looked back on those few hours that followed, he would come to think of them as among the most unusual of his entire career as a police officer.

To begin with there was silence. When Colander pushed open the door and led in Mma Ontoaste and, to a lesser degree Tom Hurst, Toff Toffsson, back on duty in reception, stared at them in open-mouthed astonishment. Then he pressed some kind of buzzer that alerted all the other police officers who up until that point had been waiting in the conference room where they met every Friday for the Ingmar Bergman Film Club. One by one they trooped out and stood in reception, making a semicircle round the two foreigners.

Mma Ontoaste tapped her clogs uncertainly and rolled her eyes. Her snakebite was suddenly aching. She wondered if an aching snakebite meant the proximity of danger. That would be a good thing for a detective to have, surely, she thought. Tom Hurst

114

checked the pocket of his reindeer leather waistcoat for the IKEA ticket. He glanced at Mma Ontoaste nervously.

It was Tord Tordsson who spoke first.

'Hello and welcome to Ynstead Police Station. I trust you had a pleasant journey?'

There was deflation all round.

'Oh Rra, it was the most wonderful journey, and to be met at the end by this handsome Swedish police officer was beyond my wildest dreams!'

The officers laughed politely and Inspector Colander blushed. Tord Tordsson turned to Toff Toffsson, fumbling in the top pocket of his uniform for his billfold. He passed him a ten-Kroner note.

'Toffsson, take this and nip down to the shops and get in a couple of cartons of Umbongo, will you? For our lady guest.'

Mma Ontoaste thought perhaps her snakebite might ache if she were about to be offered a carton of Umbongo. This was an undeniably less useful quirk, it was true, but it would always be welcome. She quickly explained that Umbongo was from the Congo, of course, while she was from Botswana, where they ordinarily drank bush tea, except that today, after such an adventure, she was very keen to try some of the local *akvavit* or the *flagg-punsch* that she had heard so much about.

'Wait a minute,' said one of the officers, shouldering his way to the front of the group. It was Nog Noggsson, secretary of the Ingmar Bergman Film Club, and a man who had always been against allowing anybody not from Scandinavia to do almost anything. He was a bulky man of about 60, with messy white hair, a lined handsome face and dark eyes. He was wearing an anorak.

'We cannot allow you into the conference room to watch the film. I am sorry but there are rules.'

Lemmingsson explained the situation with the film.

'I am still against it,' said Nogbad confrontationally. 'This is the sort of erosion of values that has let in the far Right to our country and led directly – *directly* – to the assassination of Prime Minister Olof Palme.'

The police officers shifted from foot to foot and looked askance. 'Oh, bollocks,' said one after a pause. 'Sweden's fine. Much better than most other countries, even if we never managed to solve that case.'

'Yeah, shut up, you windbag,' chimed in another. 'Always going on and on about all this stuff that never happens anyway. Listening to you, anyone would think we had one of the highest crime rates in the world and all we ever did was murder one another.'

'Yeah. Just because it rains now and again and can get dark early at night.'

It was decided that they should ignore Nog Noggsson and that Mma Ontoaste and Tom Hurst could have honorary membership of the Ingmar Bergman Film Club, so long as they were not actually watching an Ingmar Bergman film, which Mma Ontoaste thought did not really go far enough but Tom Hurst accepted on the grounds that he would probably never be in such a situation again.

Lemm Lemmingsson had done well to find two extra chairs and to arrange the room so that Mma Ontoaste sat towards the back of the room with Burt Colander on her right and Tord Tordsson on her left. Tom Hurst was given a seat on the right with an obstructed view of the television. Refreshments in the form of beer and pickled herrings were handed out, the lights were turned down, and the film was just about to begin, when Tordsson asked after Knut Knutsson.

'Has anyone seen Knut Knutsson?' he asked. Lemmingsson went off to see if he was in his office but returned a few minutes later with a confused look on his face.

'It is true Knut Knutsson may be a well-thought-of police officer from Stockholm, but he is not in his office even though his music was playing on a radio.'

'A radio?' asked Mma Ontoaste.

'Yes. An old one with a coat-hanger for an aerial.'

Tom Hurst, in the gloom at the end of the line, saw Mma Ontoaste's expression quiver.

'Oh, well,' said Tordsson. 'That is his loss. Let's watch this film that Inspector Colander has found.'

The film began. Although Mma Ontoaste enjoyed it, from the very beginning it was not clear that the film would meet with unanimous approval from the members of the Ingmar Bergman Film Club.

'Oh, that would never happen,' said one.

'No,' agreed another. 'It seems most unlikely.'

'What are they all so angry about?' asked Tofsson.

'And why has he not finished painting his face? If you are going to paint your face blue, I think you must do the job properly.'

'When will Sean Connery arrive, do you know?'

Tom Hurst could not tell with which side the Film Club would sympathise: the outlaws in the Highlands or the better-dressed Englishmen. Nog Noggsson voiced the Film Club's until that moment unspoken fears.

'A Society that lives apart, with rules of its own, that consciously rejects the norms of Society, and indeed threatens the status quo of that Society with ribaldry and song and men in tartan skirts might be the most dangerous thing Sweden could face in the future, especially if some of the members of that Society turned out to be Scotch.'

There was a mumbling of agreement.

'How would we organise ourselves to defeat such a conspiracy?'

No one could offer any sensible answer and after the film the lights went up. There was applause, but also much shaking of heads.

'I just do not think it could happen.'

'It could never happen here, at any rate.'

'It was somewhat implausible, I think.'

Tom Hurst was the first to notice that Mma Ontoaste and Inspector Colander were no longer in their seats. No one had seen them leave but they must have gone together. Tom felt a stab of panic that he had missed something. Could they be investigating while he had just been watching a film? What kind of detective would that make him?

'Perhaps he has taken her to that pizza joint on Hamngatan that he is always going to?' suggested Tord Tordsson, quite put out that it had been Colander and not he who had made the first move on Mma Ontoaste.

'I think he has been banned from there,' said Lemmingsson. 'He was always drinking too much and being sick outside the door.'

'Oh yes, I remember,' said Tordsson. 'But this is typical of Colander. He is always going off on his own at the end of his cases. It is as if he needs to prove that he is a maverick, when I believe that the charm of his work lies in the dreary day-to-day stuff.'

'I agree,' chipped in Son Sonsson. 'It is counter-intuitive, I suppose, but I think the moments when he springs into action spoil the cases he works on.'

'But how else would he end them?' asked Tom Hurst. 'It would not be very satisfying if you all finally worked out who the crim-inal was while you were sitting in this room and then all went out and arrested them, would it?'

'I agree with this man from England,' said Nogg Noggsson. 'Colander has to do something physical at the end, even if all through the case you think of him as the sort of person who, if he had been a dog, kind owners should have had him put down because he is in such ill health.'

'It is his relationship with women that is the most unusual thing about him, I think,' said Lemmingsson. 'He sort of bores them into submission.'

This caused some confusion among the police officers.

'Well, we all do that,' muttered one.

There seemed nothing more to say to that.

'Well, let's go and find them anyway,' suggested Tordsson. They found Inspector Colander and Mma Ontoaste after making a few enquiries at the pizzeria on Hamngatan, which, it turned out, Colander had been banned from, but was allowed to take pizzas away so long as he promised to behave and not to vomit too close to the front door. He and Mma Ontoaste had ordered and paid for two jumbo Hawaiians with extra pineapple and twelve bottles of beer and they had got into his car and driven down the hill towards the beach. The police officers, of whom there were by now at least 15, followed the route on foot, drawn by the sound of music and laughter.

When they found the woman from Botswana and the Swedish police inspector, no one spoke for a few minutes. All the officers stood shoulder to shoulder and stared out to sea. Below them Colander had parked the car by the beach, with the headlights pointing outwards, and in the full beam he and Mma Ontoaste were dancing to some music that none of the men recognised that was playing from the car's stereo. Eventually the song came to a stop and Colander and Ontoaste sensed their audience. They turned and faced the ring of men standing on the quayside and it was only then that the police officers noticed that the two people on the beach were naked.

'Colander!' shouted Tordsson, snatching a megaphone from the back seat of Colander's car and bellowing into it. 'You are fired!'

*   *   *

The next morning Tom Hurst woke up with a headache and a sore neck. He had slept awkwardly on the sofa in ex-Inspector Colander's sitting room and he had been kept awake by the laughing and other noises coming from across the hallway in the bedroom.

In the kitchen Mma Ontoaste was making coffee.

'Oh, good morning Rra. I hope you slept well?' she asked.

'How could you?' asked Hurst.

'I know. I am trying coffee and he is trying bush tea.'

'That's not what I am talking about and you know it,' said the Lecturer. 'I am talking about you and Inspector Colander.'

'Ah. Burt. We knew each other in College; did you know that, Rra? We were in the same year. He is a bit older than me, of course, since he was a postgraduate student.'

'I know all that!' snapped Tom. How could he forget? They had spent the entire previous evening poring over the many photos that Colander had kept of his years at Cuff College. To begin with, it had been interesting to see the Dean, then a mere Junior Fellow, and Wikipedia in their youth, but Ontoaste and Colander had gone on and on about all the people they remembered. The worst of it was that Tom was sleeping in the sitting room, where all this was going on, so that he could not say goodnight and slip away. And all the time that awful song they kept playing, 'Seasons in the Sun'.

Still. It gave Tom something to go on. His first thought was that the Dean should have told him that Mma Ontoaste and Colander knew each other. Why didn't he? Tom could not decide whether their knowing each other was just one of those strange coincidences or merely a detail the Dean considered insignificant. He would have to find out.

At this stage he was looking for reasons why they had been drawn to Sweden. The answer would probably lie in IKEA, of course, as it usually did, but it was as well to have some sort of establishing framework for this avenue of enquiry.

'But what about Mr JPS Spagatoni?' asked Tom, returning to Mma Ontoaste, who was now eating some cheese from the fridge. 'Aren't you married to him? Isn't he in hospital?'

'Ah, that good man. Well. Yes. I am married to him and he is in hospital but the chances are that he is dead by now and anyway, there is an old Botswana saying: north of Suez there aren't no Ten Commandments. Is there any beer left in that bottle?'

Tom absently passed her the bottle. She pressed the spout to her lips and chugged it back. A huge beery belch erupted a second later. Then ex-Inspector Colander emerged from the bedroom like a bear from his cave. He was wearing a pair of tight pale-blue briefs that made Tom look away and he was scratching his grey-haired chest and groaning horribly.

The flat felt suddenly very small.

The trip to IKEA was accomplished in virtual silence. Tom felt very uncomfortable and opted to sit in the back like the child that Mma Ontoaste and Inspector Colander would never have. Colander had suggested the Malmö branch of IKEA, on the road between Trelleborg and Lund, on the Cederströmsgatan and they came off into the car park at about midday.

'Just in time for meatballs!'

The Malmö IKEA is like any IKEA anywhere in the world and Tom Hurst, who up until that moment had been feeling like a stranger in a foreign land, knew where he was from the moment they went up the stairs to the restaurant and collected their lunch. Tom paid the bill, but Mma Ontoaste and ex-Inspector Colander each tried to intercept the receipt for their expenses. Colander, playing the role of the gentleman, yielded. As they took their seats, he started expounding his theory of food and detective fiction.

'Food for the detective is very important, you see, Tom. It is the easiest way to get a readership to identify with, or at least empathise with, someone who might otherwise be a slightly leaden character. Take me, for example. In most of my cases I have behaved repellently – the business of wiping my body on curtains is just one instance – but everybody knows I drink a lot of coffee and everybody drinks coffee too, and so—'

He ended his speech with a charming shrug.

'And my bush-tea habit, Rra, is famous throughout the land, even though it tastes like hog piss.'

'You have to have something, Tom, if you want to get on in this game. Swedish meatballs would be as good as anything.'

Tom speared a meatball and found that it was good.

'Oh yes, Rra. Food matters almost as much as having a side-kick. A sidekick is best if the readership can identify with them, so you have to choose carefully when you are picking a sidekick. When I think about poor old Mma Pollosopresso—'

And here, remembering that good lady, still under Botswana skies, Mma Ontoaste started to cry. Colander patted her hand and took over the conversation.

'Ideally you are after someone to whom you can talk about the case, so that you needn't go through so much tiring exposition, and then they get to know the case almost as well as you do, but importantly they must come to slightly less intelligent or insightful conclusions that your own. I use Lemmingsson for this but, to tell you the truth, I think people like my exposition. I am one of the few detectives not afraid to bore people, you see?'

Tom nodded. Mma Ontoaste was recovering herself.

'Music too matters for some of us,' continued Colander. 'I like opera, of course, even though I do not appear to know very much about it.'

'I don't like the music bit, Rra,' said Mma Ontoaste, wiping away some of the tomato juice round her lips. 'It never works because few writers are good enough to capture in writing the feeling that music creates. You can only do this through atmosphere. I like to talk about the sky, of course, and I love to repeat myself.'

This is interesting, thought Tom, but he had finished his meatballs and was suddenly anxious to get to the bedding department.

'What do you think you will do now, Rra, that you lost your job?' asked Mma Ontoaste with a caring look in her eyes. Colander took a long sip of beer as if he were even then only just making his mind up.

'If you had asked me last week I would have had only two choices: the suicide or the sauna. Now though, someone has come into my life and I think I want to change. To move away from all this Nordic gloom—'

Mma Ontoaste began blushing. She and Colander obviously had a lot in common and were enjoying each other's company. Tom would have left them to it, but he knew he would need the Inspector's Swedish when it came to tracking down the mysa måne duvet. After his third cup of coffee the ex-police officer finally hauled himself out from behind the table and they followed Tom along the yellow line, first through the bookcase section, then into the chairs and tables section, to storage and secondary storage and then the children's section.

All the while Mma Ontoaste cooed with excitement at what she saw. They lost her in the cookware section and instead pressed on through floors, pets, kitchens, kitchen decoration, furniture care, lighting, secondary storage again, and then on to sofas and armchairs, the summer tableware section and the textiles, and then to the beds and mattresses section where they finally found the bedlinen area.

'What do you hope to find here, Tom, may I ask?' asked a ruminative Colander.

Tom Hurst had not really thought about this too much. Once he had found the price tag back in Gaborone – it felt like a lifetime ago now – he had just followed his first instinct without giving it too much thought. The flight over to London and then on to Stockholm had been taken up with trying to keep Mma Ontoaste from squashing him in the competing excitements of the window and what the hostesses were doing up and down the aisles. Now, though, as he stood and surveyed all that was on offer in the bedlinen department of the Malmö IKEA, he could not think of a single thing that a duvet might tell him about who had stuck a spear in a woman in a library back in Oxford.

'Perhaps we will know it when we see it?' he ventured. Just then Mma Ontoaste pushed a huge trolley full of various pots and pans through the gateway and into the department.

'My God,' said Colander. 'And we have not been to the Marketplace yet.'

Without really knowing what they were looking for then, the three detectives began the last stages of their search for the elusive mysa måne.

Five minutes later they had given up.

'Let's ask someone,' suggested Mma Ontoaste. Colander and Tom exchanged a glance.

'All right,' they agreed and walked off in the wrong direction, consciously keeping an eye on Mma Ontoaste as she sought out an assistant. Men, she thought, would, in real life, make terrible detectives. They are always so frightened of asking questions.

She found an assistant by a computer and asked her to look up the mysa måne. As she had predicted, Colander and Tom looked over the assistant's shoulder at the screen.

'It costs 179 Kroner,' added Tom, as the assistant drew her first blank. After another couple of failed attempts the girl – no more than 25 years old – told them that there were none left in the store.

'What about Helsingborg?' asked Colander.

The woman tapped away.

'No. None there. In fact there are none in Sweden.'

None in Sweden? This was a blow.

'Well,' began Tom with a falter in his voice. 'Where are there some?'

The woman's fingers flew over the keyboard of the computer.

'They are very popular items. There seems to have been a run on them in the last week and there is only one left for sale anywhere in the world,' she said.

'Where?' asked Tom.

'Edinburgh. In Scotland.'

All three detectives looked at each other. They knew the score by now. Edinburgh. Scotland.

'Let's go,' all three said together and, as one, they turned and marched out of the store, following the yellow line back through the beds and mattresses section, the textiles section, and the summer tableware section, back through the sofas and armchairs section, the secondary storage, lighting, furniture care, kitchen decoration, kitchens, pets, floors, cookware, children's, secondary storage, primary storage, chairs and tables, bookcases and finally out into the car park.

From where Colander's had been stolen.

'Finally!' he cried aloud. 'A real crime.'

Part IV

Kernmantle
(an Inspector Scott Rhombus novel)

Chapter One

'Any idea who he is?' asked Inspector Scott Rhombus. He crouched by the side of the pool and studied the footprints in the mud. The body of the man lay face down in the black water. It was autumn and all around him the surface of the pond was choked with golden leaves that had fallen from the grand old trees overheid.

'Nae,' said the policeman behind him. 'Some kids found him this morning, ye ken? We dinnae wanna touch him 'til someone from X Division had a wee shufty.'

Rhombus stood up and looked at the policeman. Wee Shug McCormick. Bad skin, bad teeth, ginger hair and a wall eye. Christ, thought Rhombus, however did he ever make it into the force? But that was Scotland all over now, wasn't it? Always had been. Always would be.

'You did right, Shug,' Rhombus said, patting him on the shoulder. 'You did right.'

Shug looked pleased with the compliment. It was probably the first nice thing anybody had ever said to him, thought Rhombus. Meanwhile the 'paper suits' were arriving with all their equipment in steel boxes. Two of the men, wearing their white paper suits so as not to contaminate the site, began erecting a tent over the mud where they supposed the man had entered the pond.

Rhombus stood up and groaned. His back was very bad this morning. He had done something to it the night before, although he could not remember how or what.

'Ye' all right sir?' asked Wee Shug.

'Aye. It's just an old wound playing up.'

He was standing in the Queen Street Gardens East, by the old pond with its island, a large expanse of privately owned garden square, surrounded by five-foot-high cast-iron fencing. Edinburgh New Town. It was handsome, right enough, and nowhere more so than here just off Abercromby Place, but while everybody else admired the stone-fronted façades, DI Rhombus saw them as just exactly that: façades. Edinburgh kept its secrets close enough, but Rhombus had a talent for seeing just those shutters and curtains, closed doors, and locked gates.

'There's some things here you maybe want to take a look at,' he said to the lads from the technical team.

'Wha's tha', Inspector?'

'You see those footprints there? The ones with the dark stuff in them? Take a cast, will you? And find out what the black stuff is.'

'It looks a wee bit like oil, do ye no ken?' said one of the technicians, his face masked.

'Aye,' Rhombus said. 'Oil. Or blood. Check it out, will you?'

He left the paper suit looking blank and it was as he was walking away across the grass, dew staining his shoes, on his way to the police station to file his preliminary report, that the gate to Abercromby Place opened with a squeak of heavy iron.

'I say!' came a voice; thin, high, aristocratic. Rhombus turned, cursing himself for this instinctive reaction.

'You there!' the voice continued. The man walking along the path towards Rhombus was wearing a Jacquard dressing gown over a pair of silk pyjamas and the sort of slippers that Rhombus thought had gone out with the Ottoman Empire.

'Can I help you?' asked Rhombus, not quite meaning it.

'What are you doing here?' the man asked, inserting a golden-framed monocle into his left eye and patting down his already-smooth hair. Rhombus noticed he was carrying an ebony cane with an ivory knob on top.

'You there! I say! This is a private garden, you know. Not for riff-raff like you.'

'Oh, riff-raff now, is it?' Rhombus said, dangerously quiet now.

'Yes,' said the man. 'Riff-raff. Who are you and what are you doing in this garden, reserved only for *la crème de la crème* of Edinburgh Society and their dogs, don't you know?'

'My name is Detective Inspector Scott Rhombus and I am here to investigate a potential homicide. Can I ask who you are—'

The man cut him off.

'A homicide? In Queen Street Gardens East? Impossible. We simply do not allow that sort of thing. Just as we do not allow any camping. I insist you remove your tent at once.'

Inspector Rhombus sighed. It was going to be one of those days.

'There is the body of a man in the pond over there.'

'There is a man in our pond? What on earth is he doing in our pond? Is he a member of the Committee? I shall call the police if he is not.'

'We are the police,' said Inspector Rhombus wryly.

'Well, let me see him.'

'Just a second, sir,' came another voice from behind Rhombus's shoulder, female and soft and Welsh. At that moment DS Mary Shortbread appeared to intercept the man, who was heiding past Rhombus towards the crime scene.

'Thank God you came, DS Shortbread. I was about to do that man a serious injury. Find out who he is and then get shot of him, will you? Before he makes me do something I may regret.'

'Regret something, Scott? Not you. That's not in your make-up,' said Shortbread over her shoulder as she followed the man in the dressing gown towards the pond.

Rhombus shook his heid. Regret was something he knew all about. No one regretted more than Detective Inspector Scott Rhombus. You could even say that he wrote the book on it. Regret. And Scotland, of course.

Over at the pond a techie, wearing a pair of green rubber waders that came up to his waist, had entered the dark water and was now guiding the deid man to the side. When they got the body to the bank, they turned him over so that he lay on his back.

'Good Lord!' cried the man in his dressing gown, peering over their shoulders. 'Look at him! He's a tramp! A vagrant!'

There was something in the outraged voice that made Rhombus turn and walk back up the incline to the pond. Mary Shortbread was standing on the far side of the pond, staring at him as he came. He could see the thoughts crashing through her mind like guitar chords from a Mogwai gig. A homeless man found deid among all this wealth, she would be thinking. Isn't that just the sort of case that DI Rhombus likes most? And she was right. There was nothing better than when two worlds – the one rich and privileged, the other deprived and ignorant – collided.

But it turned out that he knew the deid man. It was Wee Jock 'Jocky' McTunnock®. Wee Jocky had been living on the streets of Edinburgh for as long as Rhombus had been a policeman, surviving one freezing winter after the other, and now here he was, face down in a pond in an ornamental garden in the New Town, deid. Rhombus had bumped into Wee Jock McTunnock® often enough in the past. He had stood him a half-bottle of malt on one occasion after Wee Jock had supplied him with SOME PARTICULARLY VALUABLE INFORMATION.

'I can't believe a common tramp could get in here and damage our lovely posh ecosystem! You are the police! You should have stopped him.'

'What would you suggest, sir?' asked DS Mary Shortbread reasonably. 'Should we have taken him somewhere common and let him drown there?'

'Yes, he would have hardly been out of place in any one of those schemes on the outskirts of the city, but instead here he is, lying there, clogging up our pond. I wish you to charge him with trespass. And I want the book thrown at him, do you understand?'

'Get him out of here, will you?' asked Rhombus, nodding towards the Man in the Monocle. 'I don't want to see his face again.'

Wee Shug McCormick went to take the man's shoulder.

'Unhand me, you swine!' snapped the man, shaking off the kindly proffered hand and grabbing his cane as if to separate the top from the bottom. A swordstick? Wee Shug stepped back. Not wearing his stab vest, of course.

'Do you know who I am?' he asked in a thin cold voice.

'I don't care who you are,' Rhombus said, suddenly unable to contain his rage against this man. 'If I were you, I should get out of here fast before it occurs to me that you might be returning to the scene of your crime and arrest you for the murder of Mr McTunnock.'

Instead of being cowed by the veiled threat, the man stepped back, tightened the cord of his dressing gown and regarded DI Rhombus superciliously through his monocle.

'My name is Farquhar-Farquar,' he said, pronouncing it Far-Qhar–Farquaw. 'Does that ring any bells with you, Constable? Gordon Farquhar-Farquar?'

Dougal Farquhar-Farquar was the Chief Constable of Lothian and Highlands Police. He was Rhombus's boss. This was maybe the brother, then. It was not a battle that Rhombus could win, but that fact did not stop him starting it anyway.

'Mr Gordon Farquhar-Farquar, I am arresting you for the murder of Wee Jock 'Jocky' McTunnock®. You do not have to say anything but anything you do say may be given in evidence.'

Chapter Two

When Rhombus got back to the station, it was a hive of activity. All of it stopped as he walked into the CID room. Every face turned to look at him.

'Have you no' enough work to do, lads?' Rhombus joked wryly, provoking bursts of laughter all round. DS McAranjumper tipped his heid to one side to signal trouble.

'The Boss wants to see you,' he said, shooting his eyebrows up and down and pointing upwards to her office on the floor above. 'As soon as you get in.'

'Now I wonder what that could be about, eh?' Rhombus asked rhetorically. He gathered up a few papers from his desk and began the long climb to see the gaffer.

Three hours later and DI Rhombus was at a table in the back room of the Oxymoron bar on Thistle Street. It was decked in flags and scarves in readiness for the forthcoming football World Cup. None of them were Scotch, though, since the national team had been knocked out of the 'group of death' after a tense play-off against an injury-depleted Vatican City.

'Suspended for three weeks, pending internal investigation?' asked DS Mary Shortbread, sitting next to him nursing a tonic water, aghast. She could not believe it, but Rhombus nodded and inhaled a pint of 80/-, only topping it up with a whisky chaser when the glass was empty.

'Sounds painful, doesn't it?' Rhombus joked, wiping the faint moustache of froth from his upper lip, 'but, seriously, Mary, how was I to know who he was?'

'But he looks just like his brothers.'

'Brothers plural?'

'Aye. You know the oldest brother Angus, of course. He's our own Chief Constable, but the middle brother you should recognise from the newspapers. That's Crawford Farquhar-Farquar. He's the commissioner for regional development in the European Commission in Strasbourg. A very powerful man. The other brother, Alasdair, is a comparatively humble MSP. Gordon is the underachiever, being just a multimillionaire in his own right from his SINISTER MICRO-PROCESSING factory in Silicon Glen. I think there might be another one in there, too, but I cannot remember what he does.'

'I see,' Rhombus said. 'Well, at least it means I can watch every match of the World Cup, though.'

But DS Shortbread could tell he didn't mean it.

'Work is life to you, Scott. You're a living legend, after all. There's no way you'll watch any of the matches.'

He nodded. Mary Shortbread was right. Living legend or not, work was everything to him. The only thing that kept him regular. Without it he would play the Stones all day and Dwell on his Time in the SAS.

Rhombus recalled a few bars of a song that someone had put on the jukebox. It was as haunting as it was elusive.

'We're oan the marcch wi' Ally's aarmy, We're goin' to the Argenteeen, And we'll really shake 'em up, When we win the worrruld cup, For Scoatland are the greates' fitba' team. EASY!'

A scuffle had broken out. Just which Scotch World Cup football team was the worst? 1978? 1982? Each of the successive years had a champion. A chair was broken over the back of the man who suggested 1998 and the man who supported the 2002 team had a glass broken in his face.

'I might need a favour from you,' Rhombus asked Shortbread, ducking as a beer glass flew past his ear. This was more like it, thought Shortbread, watching the glass smash on the wall above his heid.

'Anything,' she said.

'I've a meeting scheduled with Wee Wm Low McTartan this afternoon and I don't want it leaking out that I've been 'given time off for good behaviour'.'

Shortbread understood. Or thought she did. Behind her came the sound of a man being choked to death. Someone hit someone else with a pool cue.

'I'll make sure no one blabs. Why are you meeting Wee Wm Low?'

It was a good question. Why was he meeting Wee Wm Low? On the immediate level they would probably have a drink together and it was nice, occasionally, to take a drink with someone else. But on the deeper level Rhombus was not sure why he was drawn to the company of Wee Wm Low. What did such a relationship say about him? What did it say about Wee Wm Low and, perhaps most importantly of all, what did it say about Scotland as a nation? Not much perhaps, but there you are.

'There's one or two wee questions I need to ask him,' Rhombus said evasively. He lapped at his pint and was unable to hold Mary Shortbread's eye. He wondered how much she knew about the possible existence of a sinister police organisation that someone in the grip of Nordic myth-making frenzy had called The Grey Wolves.

The Grey Wolves were criminals in uniform, an organisation begun by those policemen who had spent too long on the fine line between law enforcement and law infringement. The organisation's tentacles stretched who knew how far. All the way to the top, all the way to the bottom. New recruits were as likely to be members as the Chief Superintendent himself. It was thought they were mixed up in everything from prostitution (some of them were very attractive, joked Rhombus to himself), to gun-running, drugs, booze and of course, the supply of fatty foods to minors. If anything big went down, chances are the Grey Wolves were behind it, and if it wasn't the Grey Wolves, then someone, somewhere, would have been paid off to turn a blind eye.

But it was difficult to know who they were. Could DS Shortbread be a member? Rhombus doubted it. He watched her now as she walked away, on her way back to the station. Would there ever be anything between them? People asked all the time. He had thought about it too, on those long nights when he sat wide awake, regretting the absence of a proper sidekick, regretting not having anything more memorable than a SAAB to drive around the place and, of course, Dwelling on his Time in the SAS.

He would pace his flat then, trying to resist the lure of the great pile of automotive catalogues that he had built up over the years, trying to resist the siren call of *The Best of Top Gear*, series 1–9, on video. The next-door neighbours would usually be playing their music. He had got rid of the last lot – a gay man who played Dollar records late at night – by fitting him up for dealing heroin within school grounds and the poor sod was now serving ten to twelve years in Barlinnie Jail. That had certainly learned him. He would have to come up with something new for this new lot, though, thought Rhombus, wistfully downing another pint.

After DS Shortbread had gone back to the cop shop, Rhombus

waited in the bar of the Oxymoron quietly supping another couple of pints, giving the jungle drums time to work their magic, before he heided north in his battered SAAB, down Dundas Street, only occasionally wondering if it was dangerous to drive when he was drunk enough to see two steering wheels.

'Wha' the hell? No matter. I've got four hands.'

The SASA meeting took place in a draughty hall off the Broughton Road. Rhombus let the heavy grey door slam behind him and crossed to one of the battered chairs that the coordinator had arranged in a tight circle in the middle of the planked floor. Five or six men were there already, regulars, faces tight, muscular bodies beginning to get out of condition. Each man wore a black block over his eyes except the coordinator, whose face was pixellated. The coordinator turned to Scott as he took his chair and nodded. Scott stood up and spoke.

'My name is Scott and I Dwell on my Time in the SAS.'

There was a deep mumble of sympathy from the men gathered round.

'This morning I did it five times before I got to work.'

'I feel for you, pal,' said the coordinator.

DI Scott 'Just Now' Rhombus needed these meetings just to keep himself sane. When it was bad, he attended as many as three a day and, even when it was good, he would make time for at least one a week. He needed to be able to share his problem with men who would not judge him.

He left the meeting feeling more grounded, less confused than when he had arrived. Hearing those old SAS stories reminded him he was not the only one who Dwelt. He got into the SAAB and heided out towards his appointment with Wee Wm Low McTartan in a cavernous chilled warehouse on the Dooneybridge side of Edinburgh. It was piled high with cardboard boxes, all bearing the image of a Highland piper in full regalia, and Rhombus, seeing straight now, was able to read the contents on one of the labels. Huchta-Chuchta Foods. 36 x 18 x 6 Scottish eggs[7]. Best before 07.09.09. Export only.

'Scottish eggs is it now, Wm Low?' he asked. 'Or is it Scottish Mist[8]?'

Wee Wm Low burst out laughing.

'Oh you always were a one, Rhombus. Always making your wee jokes.'

Wm Low McTartan was Rhombus's worst nightmare. He was wearing a cream linen suit that clashed horribly with his red hair, a dark shirt and tie, and he was smoking a Cuban cigar. On his lap he gripped a small ginger-haired dog that was, even now, coughing. His voice was smoky and rough and his skin was covered in green tattoos. Some men might look ridiculous in such an outfit, but Wm Low exuded naked menace. He really did.

'Cup of tea?' he asked.

'Why do you want to see me?' Rhombus asked. No time for niceties.

'Why do you always answer a question with a question?'

Rhombus shrugged.

'You've never heard of banter, I suppose?' he asked.

'A little bird tells me that you might just have some time on your hands at the moment?' continued McTartan.

'Aye. Mebbe. What of it?' Rhombus said. The jungle drums had done their work once again, he thought.

---

7 The term 'Scotch egg' has fallen out of fashion after a campaign run by the Scotch Nationalist Party who claimed 'Scotch' was offensive, and referred only to tape.

8 Same.

'I've a little project you might be interested in. Keep you busy. Stop you moping about the place. Stop you Dwelling on your Time in the SAS, if you ken wha' I mean.'

'What sort of project?' asked Rhombus.

Wm Low waved a hand to take in all the boxes that were piled about them on pallets.

'What do you know about Scottish eggs, Scott?'

'That they represent Scotland's past and, to a certain extent, her future?'

Good answer, thought Rhombus, but Wee Wm Low McTartan rolled his eyes. He stubbed out his cigar. A whorl of grey smoke ascended into the rafters. The dog coughed politely.

'Well, there is that. But as you may have read in the paper, the Food Standards Agency Scotland has banned them. Says they're too 'unhealthy', too 'disgusting', too full of E-numbers, salt, fat, pig gristle, duck beak, chicken foot, sugar, whatever. Give you botulism, salmonella, trench foot, bird flu, you name it.'

Rhombus had read something about this ban but had assumed it was a myth, dreamt up by English tabloid journalists in the pay of Peter Mandelson or someone very like him.

'Thing is, Scott, the French and Italians cannot get enough of them. All they want are Scottish eggs. *Petit déjeuner, déjeuner et dîner.* More than that, though. The Chinese.'

'The Chinese? What are they wanting with Scottish eggs?' asked Rhombus.

'Aphrodisiacs, y'ken? They think they work as well as snow-leopard foreskins.'

'And you've tried running them down the M1 and the M6 and on to Dover, eh? But you're always being stopped.'

'Aye,' agreed McTartan. 'We've lost three shipments in the past fortnight. The bloody FSAS seem to know our every move.'

He was stroking the dog rapidly now, a gelid gleam in his eye.

'So you've got a mole?'

'Aye. A mole. I have dealt with him in my own way, of course.'

'I'll not ask how you got rid of the body,' murmured Rhombus, looking at the boxes of Scottish eggs all round him.

McTartan smiled toothlessly.

'Aye. There was an accident at the production plant.'

'Christ.'

'Meanwhile the Italians and the French and the Chinese are getting desperate for their Scottish eggs and if I don't supply them—'

'Someone else will, eh?' interrupted Rhombus. Gangsters adored a vacuum, he thought.

'Exactly,' said Wm Low. 'I need to send a shipment tonight. Three lorries. Six drivers.'

'How will you get them past the FSAS?'

'This is where you come in. I have managed to get my hands on three black Marias—'

'And you are going to fill them with Scottish eggs and then drive them south, through all the road blocks, pretending they're full of hairy-arsed Scotch prisoners that the English will not even want to look at. And you want me to show them my warrant card if we are pulled over.'

Wm Low smiled.

'I'm impressed,' he said.

'There's one thing you have forgotten about,' Rhombus said. 'Even I can't drive six lorries.'

'Ah! But that is all taken care of. I have five other, how shall I put it? 'Associates'.'

'The Grey Wolves?'

'I've heard they're called that, but eh? What do I know? Any wolf is grey in the dark am I no' right?'

'Who are these fellas?' he asked.

'Oh, just you wait and see,' cackled Wm Low McTartan. 'Just you wait and see.'

Chapter Three

Inspector Scott Rhombus was drunk. A bottle of whisky, four tins of 80/- and Jefferson Airplane 'Have you Seen the Saucers' at top volume on the stereo. He was sitting in bed, duvet pulled up to his chin, trying desperately not to Dwell on his Time in the SAS. He had Dwelt on his Time in the SAS only three times so far that day – an abstinence, as far as he was concerned.

He tried to work out why was there no question mark at the end of Jefferson Airplane's song title, but had Drawn a Blank. After that, he thought about what he was doing involving himself with McTartan. McTartan had known not to offer Rhombus money, known he would refuse it, insulted. Instead the wee man had filled out a ten pound a month Direct Debit form in favour of DrinkforDrunks, a local charity that delivered tinnies to any Scot, regardless of race, creed, age or gender, who might be too drunk to get to the pub. The charity's motorbikes, with cooled compartments on the back, criss-crossed the town, delivering urgent alcohol to distressed Scotch folk everywhere.

But still the questions remained. Why was McTartan showing him the Scottish egg operation? Surely he knew Rhombus would go straight to the FSAS? Perhaps he had something on Rhombus? But what? Or was this the first overture from the

Grey Wolves? It was something that had been bothering him all day.

After he had left McTartan's warehouse that afternoon, he had rung DS Shortbread on his mobile and had her read out the autopsy report on poor old Wee Jock 'Jocky' McTunnock®. It made depressing reading, right enough, but there was something strange about it and so Rhombus had returned to walk the New Town streets in the thereabouts. Why would an old man like that simply walk into a pond? His blood-alcohol content was high, of course, but not fantastically so for a man of his profession, so it could not have been said that he was literally blind drunk. He did not have much to live for, that was true enough, but still there was something that was bothering about it.

He had later found himself on Abercromby Place. The scene-of-crime guys had moved on, taking their tent with them – which would have pleased His Nibs, thought Rhombus sourly – and leaving the gardens in peace. Rhombus walked around to find the gate he had used to get in that morning locked. He tried another. That too was locked. Then it hit him. An old guy like Wee Jock 'Jocky' McTunnock® would not have been able to get into the garden in the first place. The fence was too high for all but the most athletic to scale.

He must have been taken to the pond.

Rhombus would have to wait for the results to come back from the lab, but his guess was that someone had dragged the old man into the pond and held his heid under the water.

As he had made his way back to his flat, he had realised that the only questions that remained unanswered were the Why and the Who.

Which were pretty big questions perhaps, and neither of which he would be very likely to answer as he sat in bed getting stuck in to the cheesy-ringed outside of a carry-out deep-pan pizza and another tinny.

'Ah, what blessed company,' he said aloud, referring to his supper. Just then the doorbell rang. It was the first time that night. People were always disturbing him when he was Dwelling on his Time in the SAS. He looked at his watch and realised that it was about time for the second body to turn up.

It was DS Shortbread. Something had happened.

'The man who looked after Queen Street Gardens East has just been found deid in his sheid.'

Right on time. Rhombus gathered his coat and followed her down the stone stairs to her car.

'His wife says he's usually home by six in the evening,' she explained on the way. 'Especially when the nights are drawing in, and so, when he didn't come back, she rang his supervisor. He found the body at 8.05 this evening. Hanging in the sheid.'

'And you're only telling me now?'

'Scott, you're suspended, don't forget. It's not your case. I just thought you ought to know, that's all.'

Rhombus apologised.

'They've called in Shona McOatcake from F troop.'

'Not Wee Shona McOatcake?'

'Aye. Wee Shona McOatcake.'

'To replace *me*?'

DS Shortbread stayed quiet, concentrating on the road. As an Englishwoman she often thought it was both Rhombus's masculinity and his nationality that made him so bad-tempered.

When they got to Queen Street Gardens East, Wee Shona McOatcake was standing at the gates. An ambulance was just pulling away, its lights flashing mournfully.

'What are you doing here?' she asked when she saw Rhombus emerge.

'Why hello my sweet flower of Scotland,' he replied only semi-sarcastically, patting her on her wee heid. 'I could ask the same of you?'

'I'm here to investigate the murder of—'

'Oh, tush!' Rhombus said. 'You're here to see me.'

'Scott, I may be in town, and I may be working from the same police station as you, and I know you are on the rebound from Fiona, but I do not want you to think of me as the diving board, is that okay?'

'Not even for old times' sake?' he asked. He fluttered his eyelashes at her and if DS Shortbread had not known any better she would have said that DI McOatcake melted.

'Oh, Scott,' she gushed. 'How I miss you and your charming ways.'

'Where's the body then?' asked Rhombus, brusque now that he had what he had come for.

'On its way to the morgue,' said DS Shortbread.

'Let's see the sheid, then. Where the poor bugger was hanged.'

They crossed the lawn to a thick hedge of laurel bushes that kept the working parts of the garden hidden from sight. Typical, thought Rhombus. Behind the hedge was a large double-doored sheid of green metal. The technicians had set up some lights and the same men in masks that he had seen that morning now cast ghostly shadows into the low canopy of trees overheid. The shed was dominated by a large mower. Tools of various descriptions hung from the walls and a coil of rope from a rafter, now slightly bent under the weight that had, until recently, been hanging from it.

'What are your thoughts?' he asked DI McOatcake.

'I think suicide—'

Rhombus whirled on her.

'But you said you were here to investigate the murder?' he snapped. 'Murrrrrrrrder!'

'I'll not rule it out,' McOatcake stammered.

Rhombus nodded and began to saunter through the shed. There did not seem very much left to discover. He was just about to leave when he spotted the corner of something poking from under the seat of the lawnmower. A letter? He slipped it into his pocket before anyone noticed.

'Inspector Rhombus!'

Rhombus jumped and turned round. It was one of the technical boys.

'That sample you asked me to take this morning?'

'Aye, what of it?'

'Crude oil. A bit strange, ye no ken?'

Rhombus shook his heid and left them to it. He wandered along to the Oxymoron bar. Inside, it was thick with smoke and mumbled conversation and the delicious smell of beer mats, spilled whisky and blood. Heaven. He found a place at a sticky table and took out the letter, which turned out not to be a letter at all, but rather some kind of technical chemical report. Rhombus could make neither heid nor tail of it. He read some of it at a murmur.

'MB&L Scotland Ltd, in collaboration with its JV Partners (OHL, PGDC, POPLL and GPL) report successful testing of the QSGE-2 well as part of the HR/AP Block. Drill Stem Tests have been concluded for two zones and have produced test volumes of condensate with different flowing capacities from each zone. QSE was tested at around 428bbl/day condensate and AP at 489bbl/day condensate through 32/64' choke.'

Rhombus supped his pint.

'Now what do you suppose that's all about?' he meant the question rhetorically, but as usual with the Oxymoron bar, someone overheard him, someone who knew rather more than one might suppose.

'I know MB&L,' he said. Rhombus looked up. The man who had spoken last was a dark-haired man in his late 40s, vaguely unkempt, with dark eyes and a soft accent that Rhombus placed as being from Fife.

'They test all over the world,' he was saying. 'Looking for oil reserves, don't-you-know? What ho! Toodle-pip! Howsabout those Hibs, eh? Harharhar.'

'Wait a second, pal,' cried Rhombus. 'Did you say oil?'

'Oh yes!' piped up another voice. 'I once invested £50,000 in good old MB&L. Discovered oil and then they repaid me handsomely and now I am a very rich man indeed and I believe myself to be above the law. I am also secretly English. So there. Hoohoo!'

A chair flew through the air, hitting the man just behind the ear. Before he could spill his pint, it was snatched away to the comparative safety of the gullet of the man standing at the bar next to him but, while this man was concentrating on that pint, someone else drank his pint. Meanwhile someone wearing what looked like a ginger fright wig and a tartan skirt grabbed Rhombus by his shirt front and lifted him to his feet so that they were eyeball to eyeball.

'Hinka cumfae Kirkcudbri canifeh? Ahl hit yi oar the heid wi a caw taughtie!'

This sort of thing was always getting in the way of an investigation, thought Rhombus as his feet left the ground. He had naturally not relinquished his grip on his pint glass and he carefully drained it in a single snake-like gulp before smashing it on the man's heid. True enough Rhombus had trained for the SAS, but the heid-butt that he then delivered he had learned at his mother's knee.

'Oof!' the man cried, his legs sagging under him. Rhombus was gently lowered to the ground.

'Another pint, please, John.'

'With you in a second.'

John had wrapped his dishcloth round the neck of the punter who had invested something in MB&L and was pulling it tight. Rhombus drained the man's pint. He would not be needing that in A & E, now, would he?

Rhombus cleared the glass and the blood and three broken teeth from his table and sat down again. When his pint arrived, he turned the paper he had found in the shed over to read the reverse. Something was written in rough pencil on the back. G.F-F. G.F-F? It could only be Gordon Farquhar-Farquar, surely? The brother of the Chief Constable, the man in the gardens that morning. What had he to do with an oil company? wondered Rhombus.

He tapped DS Shortbread's number into his mobile.

'Mary,' he said once he had identified himself. 'Does the company MB&L mean anything to you?'

'No,' she replied. Rhombus nodded, his suspicions confirmed.

'I need you to do me a favour, will you?'

'I thought you'd never ask,' she replied, not managing to keep the laugh out of her voice.

'Get me everything you can on this Gordon Farquhar-Farquar fellow, will you? I have a suspicion there is MORE TO HIM THAN HE IS LETTING ON.'

Rhombus terminated the call and looked at his watch. He was due at McTartan's to meet the other members of the Scottish egg smuggling team in a quarter of an hour. As he staggered out of the bar with a cigarette stuck in his mouth, he saw two – no, four, no, two – men leaning with their arms folded against his car in the road outside.

'Ge'off ma feckin car, youse!' he shouted before realising that the two men were DI Dougal McI'lltaketheHighroad, and his partner DS Douglas Cornrig. There was something that Rhombus did not like about the way they were standing there, arms crossed, like vigilantes. He had been wondering if it was about now that someone would tell him he was a suspect in a murder case.

'DI McOatcake sent us,' said McI'lltaketheHighroad. 'You're to come to the station with us just now. Says to tell you you're in the frame for Wee Jock McTunnock®'s murder.'

'Och, boys, you're not to listen to wee Shona McOatcake. She's a gurl, fur fecksake! A wee lass!'

McI'lltaketheHighroad glanced at Cornrig nervously. Cornrig licked his lips.

'Aye, well. Okay then,' he said. 'You're right.'

Once they had gone Rhombus sat in his car for a few moments, Runrig on the stereo, thinking. He felt comfortable being in the frame for Wee Jock's death. In a sense he felt responsible for it anyway, even if he had not actually pushed the old man into the pond and then held his heid down. He was Scotch and so was Jocky. They were all in this together. It was them against the world, just as it always had been.

He turned his car engine over. A warning light on the dashboard blinked. Oil. He needed oil. What was it that man had said about MB&L? Could they have discovered oil in the middle of the New Town? And if so, who had given them permission to look for it? It looked as if he would have to pay Gordon Farquhar-Farquar a bit of a visit.

Chapter Four

Detective Inspector Scott Rhombus pulled his SAAB round the corner and into the yard of McTartan's warehouse. When he pulled up, the lights were blazing and five cars were parked over by the wall: a Maserati, a Lagonda, an Aston Martin, a Ferrari and a Lotus. Rhombus was surprised. It was like the Celtic Football Club training-ground parking lot.

Next to them were three black Marias, engines running. They certainly looked the part. He wondered where McTartan had acquired them.

And then he knew.

Round the corner came five men, all of whom he recognised: DI McTavish, DC McGreyFriarsBobby, DI McTam-o'-Shanter, DC McScottsPorridgeOats and DI McHighlandgames.

'Well, well, well, the gang's all here,' he said.

The policemen shifted from foot to foot, their wrists and fingers jangling with heavy diamond-studded jewellery. Each was smoking an enormous cigar. Who would have thought this lot were the Grey Wolves?

'Glad you could join us, Inspector Rhombus,' said McTartan, emerging from the shadow behind one of the vans, light glinting off the sovereign rings on his fingers. He was smoking his cigar and stroking that ginger dog, whose cough was getting worse.

Rhombus was to share a cab with McScottsPorridgeOats, the second van of the convoy. They would set out along the M8 towards Glasgow and then take the M74 south, where they would be met just beyond Carlisle at a service station on the M6, where McTartan had left a people carrier to bring them back in time for duty the next morning.

DC McScottsPorridgeOats took the first shift behind the wheel. He was a heavy-set man with ginger hair and skin with the texture and smell of a cheese-and-onion crisp. His friends called him Quaker, but Rhombus didn't. Instead he turned his face to the window and watched the lights pass as McScottsPorridgeOats ground through the gears, trailing the van in front of them, heiding westwards along the motorway.

The first that Rhombus was aware that it was a trap was when a line of dark blue Ford Mondeos moved into the outside lane and began travelling at the same speed as the vans. Each car was filled with burly-looking men. Then a 'jam sandwich' in the slow lane aheid began to slow down just as the three trucks were climbing up a hill by Harthill. Then the lights started flashing. There was nothing the drivers of the black Marias could do. No way out the front of the convoy, especially at the low speed they were travelling, and not enough room either side to do anything fancy.

But if the FSAS boys sprang their trap perfectly in order to check the vans, they were clueless when it came to apprehending the drivers. Rhombus jumped from his cab, tearing the shoulder of his jacket in the process, and shoved his way past one of the food inspectors. He sprinted across the run-off and up the embankment leaving the man trailing in his wake.

At the top was a wooden fence. He rolled over it, in accordance with the SAS stylebook, and ducked into a dark ditch. He had to move. Aheid was a ploughed field that stretched down to a cluster of lights. A village. He knew if he could make the lights he would be safe. He set off, skirting the field, heid kept low, sticking to cover, his training kicking in. When he made it to the line of bushes that marked the track from the field to the road, he paused to get his breath back. He scanned the field behind him.

Christ. He could make out some figures running bent double. But who were they? The FSAS boys or the police drivers?

He squatted in the bushes as the figures approached. What a disaster! Christ. And yet he could not help but smile.

'Hello, boys,' he said, standing up suddenly. 'Nice night for a walk.'

'Christ, sir, you frightened the life out of me,' muttered one of the hunched figures, hand pressed across his chest.

Ten minutes later all six of them were sitting round the circular table in the back room of The Wild Deer bar, in Hartshill, each with a pint of 80/- in his hand and a story to tell. Wee Wm Low McTartan was on his way. God knows who he would be bringing with him. Muscle of some sort, guessed Rhombus as he paced the floor in front of the fire, feeling like a child waiting to be picked up by an angry parent.

He could kick himself, he thought, for getting himself mixed up with these bloody amateurs. Wm Low would have every right to be angry. But angry with whom? Surely the mole came from within his own organisation?

A helicopter clattered overheid.

Then heidlights swept across the ceiling of the back room as a car parked in the car park. There was a thump of car doors. Rhombus counted eight of them. He raised his eyebrows.

'We've got company,' he said.

Wm Low McTartan was a dangerous man when roused. He was apoplectic now. He had just lost three lorry-loads of prime Scottish eggs.

He had brought six men with him, all of them wearing stockings over their heids, all of them carrying the sorts of weaponry Rhombus had not seen since his trip to the Imperial War Museum in London.

'So who blabbed?' asked Wm Low, once the door was closed. He was walking around behind the seated men. His ginger dog whined when she heard his voice, freighted, as a more pretentious writer might not be able to resist saying, with menace.

'Well? Who was it? One of you blabbed. One of youse told the FSAS about our wee plan. If I don't find out tonight who blabbed, then I'll have tae shoot you all.'

'It wasn't me!' blurted McTavish.

'Nor me,' said DC McGreyFriarsBobby. 'I wasnae even there!'

'Och,' said DI McTam-o'-Shanter. 'I'd never do anything like that. I hate the FSAS.'

DC McScottsPorridgeOats and DI McHighlandgames both agreed that it was not them either, and that they hated the FSAS just as much as DI McTam-o'-Shanter.

McTartan turned to Rhombus, who had been sitting quietly in the corner, looking as if he were thinking about something else, which he was. He had realised that this was all about police corruption now and he would have no time to cover illegal immigration or any of the other stuff he wanted to sort out.

'Well, well, well, Inspector Rhombus. You are awfully quiet tonight? Has the cat got your wee tongue?'

'It was not me who blabbed and I can prove it.'

'Och! Prove it can you? Go aheid. It might just be the last thing you ever do.'

'How long have we been working together?' Rhombus asked. He appealed straight to McTartan, who had to think for a while.

'Well . . .'

'Well nothing. We've got form, McTartan. These boys don't know any of the wheels within wheels, how to push, pull, bend a little. I'll bet they don't even know the name of the top Grey Wolf.'

'Yes we do!' snapped McHighlandgames. 'It's you that doesn't!'

'Let's put that to the test, shall we?' asked Rhombus, standing up now and taking from his top pocket six notebooks and six pencils. He began passing one each to the men sitting round the table. They were sweating now.

'If these men are who they say they are,' he said, 'and not police informers sent to find out about the Grey Wolves, they should know the names of everyone in their organisation, shouldn't they?'

McTartan nodded slowly, yet to be completely convinced, but interested to see where this was going.

'Now, in this book,' he held up one of the notebooks, 'I have written the names of every Grey Wolf in the police force today. You see, I know them all because I am a Grey Wolf. These men aren't Grey Wolves and they don't know any of us, so let's see, shall we?'

'I don't like this!' yelled McScottsPorridgeOats. 'I don't know what he is up to, but there's something going on!'

'Youse shut up!' shouted McTartan. 'Do as Mr Rhombus says. All of you. Write down the names of the Grey Wolves in your organisation.'

When the policemen had finished writing, one of the men in masks began collecting the books together. He passed them over to McTartan, who flicked through the first with pursed lips.

Nothing in there that he had not expected. It was McMysteryCat's book. He tossed it back on the table and flicked through another. The same thing. Then again. Finally, when he had finished, he looked up at Rhombus.

'Now compare them with what I have in my book,' Rhombus said, sliding his own notebook across the table. McTartan started flicking through the pages of the last notebook. A frown puckered his brow.

'It's blank,' he said, dropping the book with a look of fury on his face.

Afterwards there would be no one to ask Inspector Scott 'Just Now' Rhombus who it was who had shouted 'Kill 'em!', but somebody certainly had shouted it and in the split second of silence that followed before the din, there was a confused cocking of weaponry. And then it came: a roar of gunfire.

The only man who moved more than a trigger finger in those seconds was Rhombus, who, recalling his training, dropped with his face flat to the carpet, letting the roar of ordinance fly over him. A great wrench of sound seemed to tip the room on its side and threatened to deafen him. If the din was extraordinary, the smell was even worse: cordite, gunpowder, fresh blood, burned flesh, singed clothing and hair, beer and whisky all combined to remind him of some of his best nights out.

After the gunshots came the sounds of bodies falling, a short-lived scream and the sound of falling weaponry. Rhombus kept his eyes tight shut. After a few seconds all that could be heard was a horrible gurgling sound and rasping breath. Something was dripping from the table. A last body slumped to the floor with a groan of escaping breath. Rhombus opened his eyes. Bodies were everywhere. All five policemen were still in their chairs, flung by the force of the bullets to their heids. All of McTartan's men were lying on the ground, thrown back against the walls. Chest wounds. Caught by the bullets that had already travelled through the skulls of the seated men.

A basic error of positioning. Rhombus had seen it before in road ambushes when those on one side were directly opposite those on the other. By the end, everybody was deid.

Rhombus got to his feet. McTartan was clutching his chest, still alive but bleeding heavily and unable to talk. His dog coughed gently, apparently unharmed.

'Looks like you gents have enjoyed yourselves,' came a voice from the door. The landlord.

'Ah, Landlord! A pint of 80/-, please,' Rhombus said, moving aside the pulpy mess that was all that remained of McTavish's heid to retrieve the pile of notebooks. 'And an ambulance for my friends here.'

Chapter Five

Inspector Scott 'Just now' Rhombus sat in the Oxymoron bar with a pint and a pile of bloodstained notebooks on the table in front of him, deep in thought.

As he had been parking the car in Thistle Street, his mobile had rung again. He'd glanced at the number. Not one he recognised. Strange, he'd thought, holding the phone up to his ear and taking the call. It had been the Dean of Cuff College, his alma mater, before the SAS, that is. A blast from the past, all right. With the phone pressed to his ear, he'd ordered a pint with a nod to the barman and moved into the back room.

'Rhombus, old boy, I am sorry to bother you like this out of the blue, but I wonder if you might do me a favour,' asked the Dean.

'Aye, I'm not up to much just now as it goes,' Rhombus replied.

'We have a new Lecturer in Tran and Path and he has a little problem on his hands that he feels he might need some help with. I'll let him tell you about it, of course, but he's coming over from Stockholm tomorrow and I wonder if you could be on hand to meet him? He does not know Edinburgh well and I told him you might be just the man.'

Rhombus agreed.

'There is one other thing, though. He's travelling with a couple of friends . . .'

Rhombus promised the Dean he would do what he could and would even try to come down for dinner some time soon. After he had said goodbye, he ordered himself another pint and a whisky chaser. Plenty of time before heiding along the road to see Gordon Farquhar-Farquar in his New Town palazzo. After that Rhombus would be able to retire to his bed, have a bite to eat, a few more tinnies, maybe put on some Blue Öyster Cult and then finally take to his chair, where he would sleep the sleep of the just, knowing that he had done good that day.

After Rhombus had spent all his money and finished his beer, and all his hints to others had been ignored, he left the pub. It was just as a fight erupted over which Rising was the best. The '15 or the '45? Both had champions and no one had yet mentioned William Wallace or Robert the Bruce. It looked like it was going to be a long night in the Oxymoron.

He walked to Abercromby Place and pulled the bell-pull of the Farquhar-Farquar residence. Gordon himself answered the door with a smile that faded the moment he saw Rhombus.

'You,' he hissed sibilantly, Scotchly, even though he was not Scotch in any way Rhombus recognised, and even though there were no sibilants in the word 'you'.

'You are supposed to be in jail,' he snapped. 'Awaiting trial for the crime of interfering with my lawful business, a crime for which my friend Judge Angus McKillie of Krankie of that ilk will pass the death sentence and you will be hanged and then lots of rich Anglo-Scots with names like Fraser and Angus will wee on your deid body!'

'Were you expecting someone else?' asked Rhombus, raising an eyebrow at the multimillionaire. Gordon Farquhar-Farquar was dressed in a smoking jacket, black bow-tie and wing-collared shirt but no trousers. He had on only a pair of beige pants and black socks with suspenders. His shoes were patent leather.

'And what of it? Is it a crime to have a few chums around of an eve to help down a case of the finest claret known to man while outside on the streets men and women of inferior stock are being forced to drink pints of nasty 80/- or, worse, 70/-?'

Rhombus had to agree that it was not a crime.

'Nevertheless,' he said, 'I've a few questions for you about the death of Wee Jocky McTunnock® and that gardener.'

Gordon Farquhar-Farquar glanced along the street furtively.

'The thing is, Inspector, and I do not expect you to understand this, but I am expecting some guests and I don't want them to see not only a wanted murderer but also a member of what I like to call the service classes standing on my rather fine granite doorstep, so if you would not mind clearing off, that would be most appreciated. What?'

He tried to shut the door in Rhombus's face. Rhombus pushed it open and walked into the hallway, brushing aside the decadent aristo's attempts to hinder him. The floor was marble, the wood-work oak. A chandelier hung overheid and on the walls were large oil paintings of men and women who each bore a family resemblance to one another and, of course, to Gordon Farquhar-Farquar himself. A broad avenue of stairs led upwards to the promise of four-poster beds made up with linen sheets and, in the bathrooms, claw-footed baths and exotic salts.

Rhombus was distracted from thoughts about his own hallway by the sound of voices gently burbling from behind one of the doors leading off. As he walked towards the door, he heard Farquhar-Farquar groan. He smiled as he turned the handle and walked in. It was the heat that hit him first. The room was kept deliberately warm and he quickly saw why: two naked boys were holding up a flat-screened television.

On the chesterfield in front of them, watching the telly – McCrimewatch, Rhombus could not help noticing – were three men dressed in the same manner as Farquhar-Farquar.

'Yikes!' cried one, leaping to his feet, his hands scrabbling to cover his pale pink boxer shorts. He was a bulkier version of Gordon Farquhar-Farquar. Could this be Dougal? Or Angus? Or Alasdair? Or Crawford, even? One of the others – another brother – was trying to hide his scrawny thighs with an antique cushion while the other was on his mobile, ordering up yet more vintage champagne from his wine merchant in George Street.

'Who are you?' the erect one asked.

'I might ask the same question of you,' responded Rhombus.

'Well,' he began, moving forward to shake Rhombus's un-expecting and limp hand. 'My name's Crawford Farquhar-Farquar. I am Commissioner for Regional Development at the European Commission in Strasbourg. You must come out and see me some time. Call one of my secretaries and have her fix it up. I can lend you some moolah.'

Rhombus nodded.

'Will do,' he murmured.

'And this is my brother Alasdair, whom you may know already? He's an MSP. Back-bench at the moment, but you can't keep a good Farquhar-Farquar down, as Mater used to say.'

Rhombus shook hands with Angus.

'Gordon you've met, of course,' he went on, nodding at Gordon, who stood by the door, shifting from foot to foot and trying to signal that Crawford should say no more.

'Dougal is the rude one on the phone, trying to whistle us up some more of this fizz, and Angus will be with us in a second, I hope.'

There was the sound of flushing from a room next door.

'And these two lovelies are Craig and Derrick.'

Craig and Derrick nodded nervously at Rhombus. He saw their faces were painted to look like tigers.

'Boys,' Rhombus said.

'Do collapse, er . . . I didn't catch your name?'

'Detective Inspector Rhombus of the Edinburgh and Lothian Police,' intoned Rhombus.

'Oh? Then you'll know Angus? He's the Chief Constable. A devil for the boys, you know? Never been able to explain it, but Mater said that Pater was too, so there we are. Runs in the blood. Drink?'

Rhombus thanked him and took a glass. Vintage Krug. On telly, McCrimewatch had the first reports of the shooting in the Wild Deer bar in Harthill. They showed an Identikit picture of a man who had coolly ordered a pint of 80/- before driving away in one of the deid men's cars. It was a fair likeness, thought Rhombus, but it was not clear if they wanted to arrest him or reward him.

He knew he had only a small amount of time before Chief Constable Farquhar-Farquar returned and threw him out.

'I've a few questions I'd like you to answer, if you don't mind?' he asked the brothers.

'Why should we tell you anything?'

'I know you are too rich and above the law and all that, but it would save me a great deal of time and tax-payers' money if you could tell me who killed Wee Jocky McTunnock®?'

'Your appeal to my fiscal sensitivities has worked, Inspector Rhombus,' said Gordon from the doorway. 'I had my man kill him.'

'Okay,' Rhombus said, turning. 'Can I ask why?'

'It really is quite simple, Inspector. I am sure you aren't aware of this but my brother's organisation – the European Commission – takes money, in the form of taxes, from the various states of the European Union, such as Germany and Holland and France, and redistributes the money to private individuals who can afford to spend the time asking for it.'

'Go on.'

'Now because of some fiddly little regulations in place to make it look like 'A Good Thing', one has to dress up one's application for the money as if it were a sensible business proposal, so that all that any pesky lower-class journalists or, heaven forbid, policemen like yourself, might find if they investigated the request for tax-free unearned income is a trail of complicated paperwork that would defeat their frankly inferior sense of enquiry.'

'I see,' Rhombus said, stifling a yawn.

'Well, through a company I own I applied for an oil exploration grant and was naturally given trillions of euros in order to find oil in Queen Street Gardens East and stop our reliance on the *dish-dashers*.'

'And your brother is a European Commissioner?' Rhombus said.

'It saved on postage, certainly,' continued Gordon. 'But, if we found any oil, we would have to develop the field and repay the money we had 'borrowed'. Of course, we never thought we would find any. We chose Queen Street Gardens East precisely because it looked so unpromising—'

'And it was pretty handy.'

'True enough. One can see the road sign from one's desk in one's study and so naturally it was the first place that popped into one's mind.'

164

'But Wee Jocky McTunnock saw you finding the oil, didn't he?'

'Yes. Curse him. How he got in there I shall never know, but he walked in some mud and then saw his footprint fill with dark stuff. At first he did not know what it was so he tried to drink it and had to check into A & E to have his stomach pumped. Fool of a doctor enlightened him as to what he had drunk and he went around blabbing.'

'And then the gardener got his hands on the drilling report and put two and two together and came up with four.'

'Yes. So I had to have him killed as well. Devil of a job, but my man seemed up to it.'

'Where is your man, by the way?' asked Rhombus. 'I might want a wee word with him.'

'He is downstairs in the kitchen, spit-polishing my rhinoceros-hide whip, I hope.'

He waggled his eyebrows at the cowering naked boys.

'Mind if I find my own way down?' asked Rhombus.

'I imagine you will feel much more comfortable below stairs, Inspector,' Farquhar-Farquar said. 'And while you are there, will you ask him to bring up the Margaux '86? I think we're ready for it now. And you might like to help yourself to a cup of the tepid water we keep for commercial travellers too.'

Rhombus nodded to the boys and closed the door behind him. So it had come to this. Just for the sake of trillions of euros two innocent men had to die. He opened the door and set his foot on the top step. It creaked loudly, but not enough to cover the sound of some music that came swimming up the stairs at him. He had heard it before, but where? He walked down the stairs, trying to place the tune. A radio was playing on an old oak Welsh dresser. It was insistent, haunting music, coming from a radio in the corner. Rhombus stood and looked around for a moment. The room was empty. On the large deal table, one end covered in newspaper, cloths and polish and a whip. Burnished copper pans hung on the wall, porcelain dishes were piled on shelves and an Aga throbbed with heat and good smells. An empty claret bottle stood next to a crystal decanter filled with red wine. An open door to a yard, a warm breeze.

It was as Rhombus was standing in the yard that a heavy brown bottle dropped from a windowsill above and hit him squarely on the heid. Rhombus stumbled and fell to his knees. The bottle bounced and broke into a million shards on the slate floor.

When he got to his feet, he felt light-heided. Blood from the cut in his hairline poured down his foreheid, blinding him until he wiped it away. He glanced at the broken glass.

Just then he heard a bellow of rage from above. A balding, fat, Scotch man in a grubby string vest was leaning out of his window shouting down at the stunned policeman.

'Wha' the fuck've you done to my bottle, you wee fuck?' he bellowed. 'You've fuckin' well broken it, a'n't ya!'

Rhombus shuddered and turned and walked back into the kitchen. He knew he ought to ring DS Shortcake and tell her what he had discovered about Gordon Farquhar-Farquar and his man-servant, but the strange thing was that he simply could not find it in himself to care so very much.

He let himself out and began walking quickly, as if with a new purpose in life, past pubs that he might have had a slate in, past the hall where he went to his SASA meetings, past the chip shop, the Indian carry-out shop, all the way to the McPoundstretcher on Lothian Road. He emerged five minutes later with a set of wicker cachepots, a mug tree hung with eight amusingly sloganed mugs and a toilet-seat cover with matching floor mat in butter-scotch candlewick.

Soon he was back in his own flat, taking the sheets off his chair and making his bed for the first time since he could not recall when. It seemed right somehow. Radio Four played in the background. How he loved those Archers. Afterwards he ate some tinned consommé at the newly scrubbed kitchen table and looked round his flat. Cluttered with his collection of Tennant's Special tins and back issues of *Kerrang!* magazine, he saw that it was not as stylish as he had once thought, but squalid, depressing and filthy. The cachepots and the mug tree helped, of course, but it was more serious than that. He decided he must move. Rhombus turned on his computer and began searching the internet for estate agents in Godalming. He had always fancied living in Surrey, owning a little candle shop, perhaps, with maybe some essential oils on the side and, regardless of what people said about the place, some of the properties were remarkably cheap. He wondered why it was not possible to buy online. He made a donation to the Conservative Party and then went for a walk. He had never been up Arthur's Seat, but now seemed a perfect opportunity. After all, what else did he have to do?

He power-walked his way through the southern stretch of the city, ignoring the persistent drizzle. Once at the top of Arthur's Seat, all of Edinburgh was spread out below him and he sipped his beetroot and goat-hair juice contemplatively. Some people saw only the dark side of Edinburgh: each height something off which to be thrown; each depth somewhere in which to be buried. Rhombus was not like that, but he could see that the city lacked the grace or appeal of Godalming, or Hindheid, Haslemere or even Farnham.

His head was beginning to ache now. He could see stars. He decided he needed to be in bed and began walking back to the New Town. As South Bridge ran into North Bridge Rhombus began to feel nothing but gloom. On each side of the road were disgusting-looking chip shops, baked-potato shops, one-pound shops and porn shops. There was vomit and worse on most of the walls of the soot-black buildings, and the people he passed! So ugly! Ginger, and always trying to get in his way; jeering at him, their faces like fists, their tracksuited bodies simultaneously etiolated and adipose. Blue prison tattoos carved into skin the colour of whey, teeth like gravel chips.

He stopped on the bridge and looked both left and right. Left towards the castle and the north. Right towards the sea and England. No wonder so many people topped themselves here. So near and yet so far. If he stood there much longer, he thought, he would have a go himself.

When he got back to his flat he rang his mother.

'Are youse alrigh', pet?' she asked. 'You sound a wee bit strange.'

'I am fine, Mother. Absolutely fine.'

Then he drew himself a bath and had a long soak. He still felt light-heided from the bottle, but as he scrubbed away the years of accumulated dirt, he began to feel euphoric. He turned in, enjoying the feel of his nice clean pyjamas, did up the top button, happy that for once no one had rung his doorbell or even his mobile. It was a quarter past ten. Soon Rhombus was asleep, dreaming he was flying over pearly-white clouds, chastely holding hands with a young Margaret Thatcher.

Chapter Six

In the morning Scott Rhombus woke feeling disgustingly clean and uncomfortable in his bed. He groaned as he did every morning, but this was different. Whatever had happened to him the night before had worn off by now. He looked in horror at all the tidying he had done the night before. He tore his pyjamas from his scrawny body and found some old jeans in the laundry pile, which, along with a rough woollen-mix sweater that smelled of cigarette smoke, beer, vomit and cheap aftershave, he forced on. Much fucking better.

He tried to recall what had happened to him the night before. It was all a terrible blur. A blank. He went into the bathroom, a room he seldom visited except to look at his tongue in the mirror, and shrank back from the horrid material that surrounded the toilet. He closed the door on the room and retreated back into the kitchen.

Sweat seeped from his skin. He needed a proper Scotch breakfast: something sweet, calorific and artificial, something deep-fried in old fat. But he looked at the time. He had to go and meet the Lecturer from Cuff College.

In Waverley Station Rhombus had little problem spotting the arrivals. They were dressed in Scandinavian jumpers, for a start, with ugly leather hats on their heids and clogs on their feet. The younger man seemed to be leading them across the forecourt, heid swivelling, looking for eye contact. This was a dangerous pastime in Britain in general, but in Waverley Station in particular. You could just as easily find that you had commissioned the services of a prostitute for the night as have got yourself into a fight with a terrifying man with a claw hammer in his back pocket.

Still, it was not this that most struck DI Rhombus as he watched the trio as they paused by the news-stands, looking faintly anxious. It was the woman. It was not just that she was strikingly large and strikingly beautiful, drinking from a can of vandal-strength lager now, or that she was black. It was because he recognised her.

Delicious Ontoaste.

My God, thought Rhombus, I've not seen her for 20 years, yet here she is. He recalled her from the Tea Shoppe on the street just outside the Quad, the one in which his aunt worked, with her plastered thumb in the cakes all the time. He had kept that quiet all right. He wondered if she would recognise him. He had changed since then, of course. After all that Dwelling on his Time in the SAS, who would have retained their youthful bloom? He felt suddenly shy even from this distance and approached the group circumspectly.

'Are you Tom Hurst?' he asked, knowing the answer, peripherally watching Delicious as she finished her beer and crumpled the can in one hand. Tom winced as behind his ear she let out a belch that resounded through the vaulted space of the station.

'Yes. Inspector Rhombus?'

'Aye.'

It was Rhombus's turn to wince. How could anyone be so

English, he wondered, even when they were dressed like some Baltic fisherman with a leather fetish.

'Good of you to meet us. Let me introduce Mma Delicious Ontoaste from Botswana—'

'Oh Rra!' boomed Ontoaste. 'I remember you! You are a rhombus – not traditionally built, by any means!'

She let out a belly laugh that had the porters staring. Tom Hurst was confused.

'You know each other?' he asked.

'Oh yes, Rra. We were at College together. As I remember, this man spent a long time in his room alone. "Brooding" we used to call it.'

Rhombus kept a fixed grin. He held out a hand and saw it engulfed in Mma Ontoaste's, who then pulled him forward into her substantial embrace. She smelled of beer and cocoa butter and those little towels they give you to refresh yourself on aeroplanes.

'And this is Burt Colander,' said Tom absently, when Rhombus re-emerged. Rhombus did a double take. Colander was staring at him intently.

'Christ,' muttered Rhombus. 'A blast from the past.'

'Don't tell me you two know each other as well?'

'I'm afraid so, Tom,' Colander said. 'You see, the detective from Scotland and I shared a Supervisor at Oxford.'

'You were in the same year?' asked Tom, sensing the rivalry.

'Yes. Remind me, Colander, what did you get in the end?'

'Joint honours – Swedish and Empirical Detection. What about you? I recall you going off to join the Salvation Army?'

Rhombus blushed.

'SAS actually,' he corrected.

'You joined Scandinavian Airlines?' asked an incredulous Colander.

'Can we talk about old times somewhere else, do you think? Besides, we ought to get you some proper clothes.'

'But we have to get to IKEA first,' Tom insisted, looking for some sort of support from Colander or Ontoaste. None was forthcoming, but neither did they object. They seemed not to care so very much.

'IKEA?' asked Rhombus. He had heard of the shop, of course, since it had opened in a blaze of violent rage a few years ago now, but had never felt the need to visit.

They joined the queue for the taxi and, when they arrived at the heid, asked the driver to take them south towards Penicuik and the Swedish superstore. The driver looked suspicious but they piled in and set off before he could come up with any racist nonsense. Rhombus and Tom on the pull-down seats. Colander sniffed as he settled into the upholstery, thrown close to Mma Ontoaste by her weight.

'What do you drive?' he asked Rhombus, switching the reading light off and on, off and on.

'A SAAB,' muttered Rhombus.

'Ah. A Swedish car. Always the best.'

'That's not so,' snapped Rhombus.

'Is!'

'Isn't!'

'Oh stop it you two,' interrupted Mma Ontoaste. 'Anyway, cars are so old-fashioned. You should drive a cow. I drive one and she is lovely and brown.'

Rhombus stared out of the window. He was thinking about where he might get a cow. One of those long-haired Aberdeen Anguses would have been perfect. Then he caught himself. He was not that sort of detective. He investigated the dark side of Edinburgh, the seamy underbelly if you like, and the dark side of the human mind.

He could not go around on a cow, however much that might save on road tax. Besides, how would a cow handle the hills? What about cobbles?

He watched as Colander put his hand on Mma Ontoaste's broad knee. It was a proprietary gesture. Mma Ontoaste removed the hand. Well, well, thought Rhombus.

'That's the castle up there,' he pointed, addressing Mma Ontoaste. 'Maybe I'll take you later?'

Mma Ontoaste raised an eyebrow.

'I should like that—' she started.

'After we have been to IKEA,' snapped Colander, audibly and visibly hurt by Delicious's rejection.

Rhombus pounced.

'So what sort of music do you like, Delicious?' he asked with a slight nod of the heid, as if he were moving to some groovy inner beat. She frowned at him and then looked away out of the window again. Colander gave Rhombus a wintry[9] smile.

Tom Hurst was quiet, seemingly lost in thought. He kept chewing his lower lip. Could he have made a mistake, he wondered. Could the clues that the murderer left, from that spear to the IKEA label and now this trip to Scotland, really have been to the three detectives that were in the car, rather than anything else? Was there a personal connection in the game, rather than a geographical one? The news that they had all been in the same year at Cuff was news to him. But surely the Dean should have known? He would have to make a few calls.

The driver negotiated all the mini roundabouts that blocked the way to the massive blue-painted warehouse of IKEA and

---

9 Is that good or bad? Still too early to say, perhaps. I'll make this the last footnote. It doesn't really matter one way or the other.

dropped them as near to the entrance as he was able. The way seemed to be blocked by four or five enormous coaches.

'Imagine organising a coach trip to IKEA,' muttered Tom.

All three detectives jumped out of the cab almost before it stopped moving, showing surprising turns of speed, leaving Tom to pay for the ride. Which in this case was only fair. Once again the detectives followed the yellow line through the sections all the way to the bedlinen department and once again they were unable to find what they were looking for. There seemed to be no mysa måne duvets to be found.

'Perhaps we should have rung first?' murmured Tom. There was a hiss of indrawn breath. The three detectives were all shaking their heids in disapproval.

'What do they teach kids these days?' Rhombus said

'Tom,' began Colander. 'The purpose of the telephone in our business is only to complicate matters, not help clear things up. It would only have been worth ringing ahead if you could have guaranteed that someone with a distinctive speech impediment would have answered the phone and then subsequently lied to you. Then you would have had a lead, and probably a false one—'

'The best kind,' interjected Rhombus.

'—But otherwise don't use the phone.'

Once again Mma Ontoaste had to ask someone and once again the men clustered around the assistant and bombarded her with extraneous detail. The last mysa måne had been sold that very morning.

'Och,' said the girl, 'I sold it myself. To an American.'

'An American? What did he look like?' asked Rhombus.

'A wee bit crazy to tell you the truth. He was wearing an old parka and he smelled of fish.'

'Fish?'

As they tried to leave the store with Mma Ontoaste lingering in the Marketplace haggling for a cork noticeboard, a set of fifteen soup bowls and a carpet from somewhere near Turkey, Tom felt glum.

'Cheer up Tom,' said Rhombus. 'Let's get some clothes for you all and then we can all go and have a drink and a think. Does that sound good, eh big man?'

It was not clear if he was being ironic but as the taxi drew up at the Scotch Cashmere and Tartan Centre on Prince's Street, he was smiling broadly.

'This is where most Scots buy their clothes,' Rhombus said, leading the way down the stairs. Once in the shop Mma Ontoaste and Colander were quickly surrounded by sales staff who took their measurements and returned with kilts in the correct tartan within the minute. Mma Ontoaste was quickly fitted up for a rather modest Harris tweed jacket, a white ruffled shirt, strong tartan waistcoat, kilt and a pair of thick green socks with a little piece of scarlet felt cut in the shape of a snake's tongue that stuck from the fold at the top. She refused the offer of a dirk, but took the sporran and a heavy pair of black brogues. Colander and Hurst emerged a second later, similarly dressed.

'Oh Delicious,' Rhombus said, clearly and unnervingly aroused by the sight of her in tartan. 'You look wonderful. But what a shame your kilt clashes with his self's there.'

He nodded to where Colander was looking thunderously at himself in a mirror, trying to make some sort of sense of the Glengarry hat that he had been given.

'You'll just have to keep away from one another won't you?' Rhombus laughed. Colander tore his Glengarry off and threw it on the ground. Rhombus had bought himself a blue Tam with black and red dicing and an orange pom. He pulled it down over one eye and was giving Delicious a piratical look when something she said stopped him in mid stride.

'What did you say?' he demanded.

She had been searching through the pockets of her new jacket. She looked puzzled.

'I said this one is big enough for a notebook.'

Rhombus put his hand to his heid.

'Notebook!' he said. 'The notebooks!'

All three detectives and the shop assistants stared at him.

'I had some notebooks. Five of them. Covered in blood. Christ! Each one is a list of the most corrupt policemen in the country.'

'Where are these notebooks, Rra?'

'Christ knows. I left them somewhere. They could be anywhere. Oh well, let's forget about it. They probably don't matter anyway.'

Colander stepped forward.

'You cannot mean it. If there are corrupt officers in any police force we must root them out. Get them out so that they can become security guards and make their fortunes running drugs to innocent Swedish children in nightclubs.'

Delicious looked at Colander with that gleam in her eye again and Tom sensed there was more than a desire for justice in his speech. He was challenging Rhombus: whoever finds the notebooks wins the girl.

'Where did you last see them?' asked Colander, beginning to see that he was at a serious disadvantage. Rhombus scratched his heid, beginning to see that he was at a serious advantage.

'Can't remember,' he said.

'Think,' Colander said.

'You must try at least, Rra,' Ontoaste weighed in. 'Where did you get these notebooks?'

'Jenners. There was a deal on. Six for the price of two.'

They all agreed that this was good value.

'But it does not get us much further forward,' Tom said. 'When did you write the names in them?'

Rhombus explained how he came by the names.

'Ingenious, Danny Boy,' Colander said through gritted teeth. 'But then what did you do with them?'

'I drove back into town and stopped at a pub – the Oxymoron on Thistle Street.'

'And then?'

'And then I can't remember a thing.'

It was true. He had no recollection of anything that had happened since. But since when? He could not even remember that.

Chapter Seven

'Well,' Mma Ontoaste said with a crowning smile. 'We had better get to the pub, hadn't we?'

'It's a bit early for me,' mumbled Rhombus, glancing at his watch.

'Yes,' agreed Colander. 'I like the drink excessively only when it is dark.'

'For fuck's sake,' Mma Ontoaste snapped in a rare show of ill-temper. 'It's enough to drive a woman to drink. All right. I'll go.'

She fastened the leather buttons of her tweed jacket over her substantial bust and looked at Tom.

'You coming?'

Tom shrugged. He wondered if he could safely leave Rhombus and Colander alone together.

'Actually, I fancy a drink after all,' Rhombus said, slightly shrilly.

'Me too,' muttered Colander.

'Right,' smiled Ontoaste triumphantly. 'Let's go.'

They marched out of the Scotch Tartan and Cashmere Emporium and up the hill to Thistle Street. The Oxymoron, normally a hubbub of noise, broken glass and flying teeth, became stony quiet as they pushed open the doors and ordered their drinks.

One of the barmen stopped spreading the sawdust they used to soak up the blood and stood up, rolling his eyes as if to wonder why he bothered.

'Two pints of best with whisky chasers, please, Landlord and two lime and sodas.'

The silence lasted a beat before the spit and insults started to fly. Seconds later, the four detectives were backed into a corner swatting away bar stools and pint mugs with their heidgear. A line of angry Scotsmen was trying to get at them as a pack of dogs might attack a bear.

'It's funny how none of us carry guns, don't you think?' asked Colander, ducking quickly as an ashtray flew at his face.

'And yet some of the best detectives do, don't they?'

'But, Rra, they only use them to get people to tell the truth towards the end of the case. I think it's a bit of a cheap shot.'

'We should get out of here,' shrieked Rhombus. Glass shattered overheid. A rolling soundwave of unintelligible swearing broke over them.

'Don't you want to get the notebooks, Rra?' asked Mma Ontoaste, right-handing one old codger who was trying to get a sneak up her kilt.

'Maybe another time?' whimpered Colander.

'There is no other time,' Tom shouted. 'We've got to get to IKEA after this!'

'But it's late closing tonight. We can always go later.'

'I can't believe you two!' said Mma Ontoaste. 'And you call yourselves police officers?'

At that Colander grabbed a man in a wrestler's hug and bit into his ear. Rhombus ripped the picture of the urinating dogs from the wall and smashed it over the heid of another assailant. Tom Hurst gave another a rabbit punch. Mma Ontoaste had removed her shoe and was brandishing it like a *knobkerrie*. The tide was definitely turning.

Spotting a gap, Mma Ontoaste dropped her shoe and surged forward, sweeping her assailants before her like a great black-and-tartan tidal wave. She pushed them to the double doors and shunted them out into the street. Five or six men dealt with in a second. She locked the door and returned to the bar, where Rhombus, Colander and Tim Hurst were righting chairs and dusting themselves down. The other regulars were gulping back the vanquished men's pints.

'Nice work,' said the barman as he poured her a pint. 'Don't suppose you fancy a job, do you?'

Mma Ontoaste laughed. She would not mind settling down in Edinburgh, she decided. It had a nice familiar feel about it, and a job chucking out in the Oxymoron would keep her in enough money for the foaming mugs of 80/- that she could already see herself enjoying. She would have to think about it.

'Actually, you know, hen,' continued the barman. 'I think I can dig out a carton of Umbongo? If you'd prefer? If you worked for me, we'd get it on draught, of course.'

'Rra,' she said, wiping the froth from her upper lip. 'Umbongo comes from the Congo, as you must know, while I am from Botswana.'

'Oh, aye, good point.'

'Now my friend here believes he may have left some notebooks in here the other night. He says there were six of them, covered in blood.'

'Blood, you say?'

'Rhesus negative.'

'Could these be them?' he asked, digging behind the bar and finding the notebooks, crisp with dried blood.

'Well, that was simple,' said Tom.

'What do you mean, simple?' chorused the detectives. Mma Ontoaste looked especially pleased with herself at having solved the case.

'You know we had a case like that in Ynstead once,' Colander said. 'A schoolchild left her herring on the bus. We tracked it down, though. Police procedure. Getting the men out there, knocking on doors, asking questions.'

Nobody said anything for a minute.

'Right,' said Tom eventually. 'Shall we have a look at them? Find out who these corrupt officers are?'

They took a book each.

'I've got someone called DI Stony Creek,' Colander said. 'Maybe another one of your amusing nicknames?'

'Shit Creek would be an amusing name,' Rhombus said. 'But not Stony. Beside there's no Creek in the Scotch police We only allow Mcs or, at a push, Macs.'

'I've found a Marion McKenney?'

Rhombus shrugged. He had not heard of her, and he had been out with half the female police officers (and one male, but that was an undercover job) in the force.

'Dilwyn Dumfries?'

'Clifton Forge?'

'Can we have another two pints please, Rra?'

None of the names meant anything to Rhombus.

'A code, then,' Tom sighed.

'A what, Rra?'

'Never mind. We will have to try to break the code. Find out what the names mean.'

He found that, when he spoke to Mma Ontoaste, he slightly raised his voice, as if she were simple or something. He got out his blackberry and began putting the names into Google. First he tried Dilwyn Dumfries. Nothing. He removed the inverted commas. Lots of information about antecedents with the surname, but nothing concrete, nothing immediately obvious. Then he tried Elkton Edinburg. It was an unusual name. Again, nothing certain.

'Just hotel reservation sites for places in America.'

'There's a hotel called Elkton Edinburg over there?'

'No. It's two place names – in Virginia.'

He tried another and stared at the results.

'Cliftonforge.org,' he said.

'Who is Clifton Forge?'

He clicked the link.

'Another place. In Virginia again.'

Tom could feel the hair on his collar stand on end. This was the thing. Virginia. He tapped in another few names. All of them were towns in Virginia, USA. What Tom could not decide was whether this was a clue that would lead him to find out the names of the bad apples in the barrel that was the Edinburgh and Midlothian Police Force, or whether it was a clue that would lead him to find out who killed Claire Morgan.

The latter, he hoped.

Part V

Unnatural Presumption
(a Dr Faye Carpaccia investigation)

1

Dr Faye Carpaccia is mixing a marinade of olive oil and lemon juice and some fresh thyme leaves in a small glass jar and outside it is unseasonably hot. Black thunderheads are beginning to build up like angry fists, masking the heat of the sun and as Dr Carpaccia crosses the room in which she is making the marinade, she decides that a storm will come.

She places the bottle of marinade on the gleaming steel surface, next to the body of the chicken that is stretched out on a gurney, naked and hairless now, ready for the Y-incision that Dr Carpaccia will make with one of the knives that her assistant has already prepared and laid out in a neat row where she can easily reach them.

Dr Carpaccia is a small woman, a very small woman, but she is a powerful woman and an elegant woman in her midnight-blue trouser suit, and she is very very kind, with a heart of gold that means she would do anything for anyone, although, in her own way, she is very reserved and does not like to talk to people she does not know unless they are dead.

Before Carpaccia touches the knives she politely nods to her assistant, a woman of Mexican extraction, with few prospects in life and a mass of dark hair that she is wearing scraped back into a hood. Along with the hood she is also wearing the standard uniform of purple scrubs, gloves, mask and safety goggles. She knows that when Dr Carpaccia gives her that nod, it means that she must turn on the ATMT Lite MP3 digital recorder that stands athwart an oaken shelf off to the left of the suite in which they are about to conduct the operation on the chicken, and this she does. Instantly the blue light that signals that the machine is working blinks on.

Standing by the bank of sinks against one wall is Detective Rambouillet, the investigating officer. He is dressed in black from his *Cats* the musical baseball cap to the Muji flipflops on his black-socked feet. He is a big man, and his big presence seems even bigger than usual in the cool air, so that Dr Carpaccia does not mind so much any more that he makes her feel even smaller than she used to feel, even in her own suite. He is chewing gum and looking bored and tough at the same time. It is a look that Carpaccia knows he adopts when he wants to hide the fact that his mind is whirring like a hamster in a hamster run, even though she has never owned a hamster or a hamster run or even seen a hamster in a hamster run.

Dr Carpaccia works her hands into a pair of surgical gloves and she begins to recite the words that she knows by heart now, having said these same words every week for almost ten years:

'The subject is an approximately three and one half pound Caucasian female chicken, exhibiting evidence of a ritualistic beheading.'

Dr Carpaccia looks up and catches the eye of her assistant over the width of the gurney. Behind the super hi-spec PSVU glass of her hybrid goggles, Carpaccia can see that there are traces of tears she is endeavouring to blink away. Dr Carpaccia can also see the admiration in the woman's eyes and knows that this admiration is aimed at her and her alone.

186

Dr Carpaccia cannot afford to be distracted by the misplaced sensitivities of her staff and she returns to look down at the chicken on the gurney before her. She nods once again to the assistant and, together on the count of three, they move the bird onto one of the steel examining tables that occupy the centre of the suite in which they are carrying out the operation.

Even through the thin latex of her powdered surgical gloves, Dr Carpaccia can feel the chill of the bird's cold dead flesh. Rigor mortis has come and gone and the forelimbs of the chicken are responsive to digital manipulation.

Carpaccia estimates the time of death to have been no later than three days ago. This conclusion is backed up by the sell-by date printed on a label found on the material in which the chicken was discovered and which is now sealed into a slim clear plastic evidence envelope that is resting on the gleaming surface of another of the steel examination tables.

'How was the subject found?' she asks Detective Rambouillet.

'Same as the others,' he replies. 'Lying on her back, with her wings and legs tied together with the same kind of twine in the same kind of knot.'

'Was it preserved?' she angrily asks.

'Jeez, Doc, I dunno,' he sarcastically responds. 'Of course it was preserved. Along with the wrapping which we found all over her body. A kind of plastic. And a weird rectangle of paper – also a bit plasticky – that the body was sitting on, and underneath that there was a cradle of pressed blue cardboard. It's all in there, tagged, in the fridge.'

He nods to one of the four walk-in fridges in which they keep things at a constantly cold temperature.

'What about the internal organs?' she mollifiedly asks.

Rambouillet nods his big head towards a bag on another gurney.

Carpaccia crosses to the other gurney and picks up the bag and opens it with a pair of scissors that she takes from a drawer. She up-ends the contents of the bag into a copper bowl with a wooden handle attached and sets aside the empty bag. Inside is a mush of dark bloody material that includes the chicken's liver and kidneys, as well as a long section of bone covered in flesh upon which the skin is still identifiable. Absent are the feet and the head.

The smell is something that Dr Carpaccia has long since gotten used to. In fact, as she introduces a foot-long wooden-tipped instrument into the bowl, she is happy with what she sees. This is one of the things that has made her the most respected figure in her profession, the sort of figure whom people stop in the corridor to obtain an autograph and to ask advice on such matters as flying helicopters, scuba-diving, vodka sauce and directions to the nearest rest room. She is always polite and she never takes offence when she is stopped in the corridor and asked this sort of question, even when it is abundantly clear that she is not the sort of person who should be stopped in the corridor and asked any sort of question by an elderly person or an ugly person or by a person who simply does not possess very much money.

Dr Carpaccia reaches for a wooden pepper mill that she keeps on a tray along with other condiments and chemicals that she will use during the operation. She takes the top of the pepper mill with her right hand and the bottom with her left hand and she turns them against each other, one counterclockwise, the other clockwise. Instantly from the bottom of the mill flakes of pepper emerge and fall blackly into the bowl. Next she adds a thumb-sized lump of yellow butter, a pinch of sea salt and eight fluid ounces of an ordinary Merlot that she retrieves from a bottle on the gleaming surface. From one of the eye-line cupboards above her she takes a bay leaf from one jar, and an imported *bouquet garni* from another. These she also adds to the bowl, which she then sets aside over a low heat while she returns to the body of the chicken.

Still no one has spoken. Dr Carpaccia likes to work in silence and Rambouillet has learned not to break her concentration with any questions. He has complete trust in Dr Carpaccia.

'So whaddya reckon, Doc? Is it the same man? Same MO?'

He is referring to the *modus operandi*, the way a compulsive murderer goes about his business.

'I won't know until I open her up,' Carpaccia says, nodding at the chicken body. Only her voice betrays the emotion she feels. She takes a deep breath before gently parting the legs and wings of the bird. Rambouillet has stopped pacing the terracotta-tiled floor in his flipflops and is staring at what she is doing, his breath held, waiting for some signal. Her assistant, the Mexican woman in the pale purple scrubs, is nervous. She has drawn her breath too, and her dark eyes are wide with terror. This is the first time she has worked with Dr Carpaccia.

After a second Carpaccia looks up and nods to Detective Rambouillet. Dr Carpaccia has confirmed what they suspected from the moment Rambouillet had called her on his cell phone from the market to tell her that he had found another body in the chill cabinet.

The chicken has had her internal organs removed.

There is a thick silence in the room.

'I don't suppose we gotta name, either, do we?' asks the detective.

Carpaccia shakes her head. This is what hurts most. The anonymity. It is up to her to make this dead chicken speak to her as she had never spoken to a soul while she was a living chicken. It is up to Carpaccia to get her to tell her story, so that the wrong of her death could be made right and the evildoer could be PUNISHED.

Afterwards, in the privacy of her study, Dr Carpaccia can let some of the emotion show, but for now she must continue with the operation.

Her assistant has passed her a Petri dish of some of the butter-yellow emollient they use as a humectant to increase the water-holding capacity of the body's *stratum corneum*, as well as to provide a layer of oil on the surface of the skin which further slows water loss and thus increases its moisture content. Dr Carpaccia takes some of the emollient on her hands and rubs it all over the chicken, paying particular attention to the thin skin of the breast. When that is done, she collects the husks of the lemon she had previously had her assistant squeeze dry and these she inserts into the cavity created by the removal of the internal organs. In addition to the lemon halves, she carefully inserts two cloves of garlic (skin on), and while her assistant holds the chicken upside down, a handful of thyme leaves and stalks and a generous scoop of salt and another extensive grind of the pepper from the mill she had previously used. There is a risk of cross-contamination, which is why Carpaccia is so careful.

Her assistant returns the chicken to a special body dish and again Carpaccia leans over and applies the salt-and-pepper coating. The crystals of the salt and the dark flakes of pepper stick in the butter and it is true to say that the chicken did not look as good as this when she was alive.

Carpaccia nods at her assistant.

'Is the OVEN ready?' she asks, referring to the Occluded Vector Electron Neuroscope that needs to be pre-heated to gas mark eight before it can successfully treat the chicken's body. From the outside all that is visible of the oven is a set of dials and a steel-framed laminated heatproof hinged-glass window.

Unnatural Presumption (a Dr Faye Carpaccia investigation)

The assistant nods. The OVEN is ready. She opens the door and a wave of heat emerges like a physical force. The assistant backs away slightly, but Carpaccia is used to the heat. She has done this too often, she thinks.

Together they wheel the gurney to the OVEN and then, again on the count of three, they pick the chicken up in her special Teflon-covered body dish and slide her into the OVEN. Carpaccia's Mexican assistant closes the door and Carpaccia checks her Rolex watch, a gift from the grateful people of Bratislava.

A tear snakes its way down the smooth cheek of the doctor as she removes her gloves and balls them into a flip-top bin that she keeps for just such a purpose. She retreats along the corridor of the Facility to her study, where she sits at her desk and bites her knuckle, desperately fighting against the feelings that well up inside her, fighting the darkness.

In her career to date Dr Carpaccia has seen some horrific sights and she is all too aware of what a damaged human being is capable of, but this case touches her deeply. The chicken is so young, so full of energy, with so much to give. She still has her whole life to enjoy. Or not.

2

Detective Rambouillet knocks on Dr Carpaccia's ash-framed door. He is holding two Styrofoam cups of coffee. It is 3.30 in the afternoon and outside the storm that Carpaccia had predicted seems to have not materialised, but it is still hot in her study and she can feel the heat pressing down upon her head and upon her shoulders as if it were a living thing.

'So what we got?' Detective Rambouillet asks. He places the cups on the desk and sits heavily down in the chair opposite her.

He seems not to have noticed that Dr Carpaccia does not like milk-free coffee and this hurts her, because she knows how he takes his coffee, so why should he not know how she takes hers? Once again she considers firing him. But he leans forward now and pours a sachet of refined sugar into his own coffee cup. He knows this is not good for him, and that it will make him sweat later on when he feels the sugar rush, and that it will make him fat and out of condition, but he does not seem to care and goes ahead and does it anyway.

They are sitting in Dr Carpaccia's red satinwood-panelled study. On the wall behind her is her extensive collection of what she humorously calls 'sheepskins': diplomas from various universities including The American College of Addictionology and

Compulsive Disorders, based in Holy Toledo, Utah, and the New Hope Bioresonance University of Holistic and Drug Free Medicine based in a small but pleasant suburban villa in Maryland.

'Is it the Butcher?' Rambouillet asks taking a good long slurp of his coffee. Carpaccia forces herself to concentrate and she nods and wishes that she had not so recently given up smoking. At times like this she misses her ex-lover, who was killed in the line of duty – the one with the strong warm tongue, who kissed and touched her, but fatally fell into the fire at the FBI clambake. Or was that another lover? She cannot recall.

'So how'd he find her?' Rambouillet asks. It's a cop question. Not one that Dr Carpaccia is qualified to answer, but she has let herself become involved. She shrugs.

'Until we know who she is,' she says, 'we won't know for sure how he found her.'

'But you got your own theory, right?' the burly detective asks.

Dr Carpaccia is once again startled by Detective Rambouillet. These are the moments during which she knows that she will not fire him. These are the moments she knows that she does not have the power to fire him. He knows her too well. He knows that she has a theory about how the killer found his victim. He knows that she does not have the power to fire him, since his pay comes from someone else's budget.

'Any matches on the FMP?' he asks. He is referring to the Fingerprint Matching Processor, a high-speed computer that is capable of comparing 800 fingerprints a second.

'Chickens do not have fingerprints,' she calmly explains, thinking that these are the moments when she perhaps she ought to fire him.

'Good point, Doc. And anyway, even if they did, there's no

guarantee of a match. I mean she mightn't ever have committed a federal crime and had her ten prints taken, might she?'

The FMP is a wonderful invention, Carpaccia thinks; capable of matching a fingerprint taken at the scene of a crime with any other print ever taken by the police, but then again when did it last solve a case? She tries to imagine herself coming back from a crime scene with a smudged print, feeding it into the computer, getting a match, calling Rambouillet or someone very much like him on the cell phone and have them go over to someone's house and arrest that person. It might happen in real life, she supposes, but – she stops. She has no idea how to finish that sentence. It might take her to a very dark place. Successful, run-of-the-mill police procedure is not what Dr Carpaccia is about.

Rambouillet is explaining his own theory about these machines.

'I call 'em RHGs,' he is saying. 'Red Herring Generators. You use some fancy piece of machinery and it tells you some damn thing that you could have guessed anyway. That freaking wand full of sea water you're always waving around? What's it ever told you? Some guy uses soap. So what? So does everybody else, but now you're all gussied up about soap. You overlook the important things like hockey masks, chainsaws and hard-ons.'

'Can we just go through his MO one more time?' Carpaccia calmly asks, ignoring him. 'So we can be really gory?'

'Right,' Rambouillet cautiously agrees. 'Well, like last time, he probably got in through the door.'

'She left her door unlocked?' Carpaccia incredulously asks. It was always through an open window or an open door. An open window is an open invitation, Carpaccia thinks. How soon would it be before compulsive murderers would be able to use the open window as a defence, just as molesters do with short skirts?

'Probably open,' Rambouillet emphasisingly says. 'Although we haven't exactly traced who "she" is yet. I've put out an APB on her and contacted the Missing Chickens Bureau but we don't have a lot to go on. Without the head, you know?'

Carpaccia nods.

'And there is no sign of it?' she asks. 'Or her feet or her intestine?'

Rambouillet shakes his head and leans forward to remove a notebook from his back pocket.

'Do you have the time to speculate on what the Butcher might do with the head?' he asks.

Dr Carpaccia glances at her watch. She is a busy woman but can usually make time to speculate on such matters.

'I think he may stab them in the eyes with school compasses,' she begins. 'And then stop up their nostrils with a waxy substance that glitters under SEM, then put lighted matches in their ears and pluck out their tongues.'

Rambouillet takes a deep breath. He hates it when Carpaccia talks about Scanning Electron Microscopy, although he cannot really figure out why.

'Okay,' he cautiously agrees. 'Is this done before or after he has chopped the heads off the rest of the body?'

'Whenever. Both. It doesn't matter.'

'So why does he do it?'

'Because he does not want them to see how small his penis is,' she calmly states.

This is too much for Rambouillet. He folds his notebook up with a snap.

'Okay,' he says after a pause. 'Back to the MO. We know that the man – and I'm assuming it is a man – whom the newspapers have come to call the Butcher, enters his victim's coop through an open door. Then he takes his victims by their feet and he hangs them from an S-hook. And then he slits their throats, right?'

'Yes,' she answers his question. 'With a lateral incision through which they exsanguinate.'

'Right,' he interrupts. 'Exsanguinate.'

'Have we any news on the blood?' she coldly asks, trying to ignore his dig at her needless use of technical jargon. For a second the idea of having him fired flits back and forth across her mind again like a silk stocking blowing in the wind. Not that, she ought to state here and now, she has seen or heard of any such thing and is in fact puzzled by what sound such a thing might make. Nevertheless, Rambouillet admits that they have had no luck in finding the blood.

'It could be that he lets it drain away but my guess is that he finds some sort of use for it. All we have to do when we find it is get a DNA match.'

They continue to discuss the Butcher's MO. Once the Butcher has let his victims bleed to death, he removes their feathers until they are bald and then he makes a vertical lateral cut from the pubis to the breast bone and he pulls out the intestines and the internal organs.

Dr Carpaccia stares out of the window as Rambouillet talks. The rain has come now and water is running down the outside of the window. It is dark, despite the lights.

'. . . We're yet to find the intestines,' Rambouillet is saying. 'But he puts the kidneys and the heart and the neck back into a plastic bag, which the sick badger then knots, and then he inserts the plastic bag into the cavity of the chicken.'

There seems nothing more to say for a minute and they sit in silence, comfortable with one another, thinking about the dead chicken until the phone rings.

Carpaccia picks it up and snaps into the receiver.

'I thought I told you I was not to be disturbed?'

She is good and kind, if not a whole barrel of laughs, but she will not tolerate people of lesser importance disobeying her. The voice at the other end is given five seconds to explain why they have put a call through or else they will be bundled into the back of a car and taken to a crocodile swamp that Dr Carpaccia's Creepy Lesbian Niece keeps expressly for this purpose in Florida. The voice, high-pitched now, explains that it is the Dean of her College.

'Which one?' Carpaccia asks, genuinely puzzled. Could it be the Dean of the University of Spectrology and Forestry, Palmer's Green, she wonders, a man whom she did not imagine to exist? When the caller is put through, she is surprised to hear a British voice on the end of the line. She had expected the usual Romanian accent. It is the Dean of Cuff College in Oxford, a college from which she was sent down for bringing adverbs back to her rooms after midnight.

'What can I do for you, Dean?' she politely asks.

The Dean sounds almost apologetic as he explains that a murder has been committed and the killer has left a trail of clues that one of the lecturers, a man called Tom Hurst, believes links him to Richmond, Virginia.

'I'm not in Richmond at the moment,' Carpaccia straight-awayly tells the Dean. 'So I really don't see how I can be of assist-ance.'

She replaces the receiver.

'Those British,' she says. 'They are all in denial.'

Had the Dean but known it, he had called at a bad time in Anglo-Carpaccian relations. Carpaccia's proof that the Second World War was really won by Dick Van Dyke disguised as Winston Churchill has been critically mauled by *The Times* of London. There is an urgent knock at the door and the Mexican woman, who has removed her mask and goggles, but is still wearing her scrubs, which is something that Dr Carpaccia would never do, puts her head round the corner of the door. She addresses Dr Carpaccia.

'Dr Crapaccia,' she irritatingly and quite incorrectly states. 'You had better come quick. There is a problem with the evidence in the walk-in fridge.'

Carpaccia and Rambouillet exchange glances. This has a familiar ring. They get up from their chairs and follow the Mexican woman, whose name Carpaccia thinks is Carmen, down the corridor to the cooking suite.

The Mexican woman is flustered. When they reach one of the three walk-in fridges she cannot speak very clearly and jabbers in a strange foreign language.

'Calm down,' Rambouillet aggressively snaps. Carpaccia thinks that she would not talk to staff so rudely and once again she wonders about firing him.

'What is wrong, Carmen?' she most non-aggressively asks, and she slaps the woman across her cheek with the back of her right hand. The ploy works and the woman calms down almost at once.

Carmen, whose name is really Juanita, explains something about someone mixing up the evidence tags so that the evidence bag that she has just placed in the walk-in fridge, which included the sell-by date label of the chicken on the gurney, now reads as if it were placed in the walk-in fridge some time last week. Getting the labels mixed up can happen, but it is a complicated and uninvolving process and all that you really need to know is that it happened and that Carpaccia and Rambouillet and the others can no longer be sure that the chicken in the OVEN is not past its sell-by date.

This in itself is not so bad, but if it leaks out to the newspapers that this sort of thing is happening in her suite, it might cause a scandal and unfairly bring Dr Carpaccia down from her position at the top of the heap, which is always vulnerable because she is a woman and some people would stop at nothing to see her fired. Someone somewhere might even wish to ruin Dr Carpaccia's career and reputation.

So the real problem is that this someone may have switched the labels deliberately and Dr Carpaccia ought to find out who this person is, and why they did it, or her tenure as chief might well be curtailed.

3

'May I see the tag label?' Dr Carpaccia is politely asking Juanita. Juanita turns and leads her and Detective Rambouillet into the walk-in fridge in order to show them the tag label, but once they are inside the walk-in fridge, in which there is enough space for three people to stand quite comfortably, Juanita looks stunned as she stares at a gap in the shelves.

Along the walls glass shelving is fronted with white plastic covering and on the shelves are various tins and jars and plastic evidence bags. Overhead a fluorescent light buzzes and against one wall is a blue filament designed to lure flies to their death.

'Oh, Dr Crapaccia,' she wails with a trembling finger out-pointing. 'The evidence! He is gone! Someone must have stolen him! Aiyeee! All is lost.'

Once again Carpaccia slaps the Mexican lady and this calms both of them down somewhat.

'Have you seen anyone in the suite apart from Detective Rambouillet or myself?' she calmly asks the weeping illegal immigrant. Juanita shakes her head and continues to sob. Carpaccia instinctively knows that they will get no more information out of her.

'I left the room,' Juanita is telling Detective Rambouillet, 'to go to the little girls' room for a minute. When I came back the window was open.'

She points across the suite to where a window has been opened. Immediately Rambouillet makes a call on his cell phone.

'Secure the perimeter,' he snaps. 'Don't let anyone in or out unless I say so.'

He turns to Carpaccia.

'Let's go check the security cameras.'

As they walk down the corridor towards the basement and the communications room, their steps ringing on the tiled floor, it occurs to Carpaccia that the confusion over the tagging of the evidence might have worked in their favour. Whoever had broken into the walk-in fridge had taken the wrong evidence. All Carpaccia had to do was find the right evidence. It must carry powerful clues to be worth the risk of breaking in and stealing it. Juanita's mistake had effectively saved a crucial piece of evidence, although this piece of good luck would not save her, since Carpaccia had already signed her cards and the Immigration Service would be stopping by to take her away in the back of a white flat-bed Ford even before her enchiladas hit the plate that evening.

Rambouillet stops and taps a series of numbers into an electronic access pad set at chest height in the beige-painted cinderblock wall. A red light blinks green and there is the sound of a bolt being withdrawn. Rambouillet opens the door. Inside is the communications centre that Dr Carpaccia's Creepy Lesbian Niece has devised. It cost more than a successful moonshot, but it allows *CSI: Miami* to be shown in every room in the Facility.

In addition, it has the most advanced centrally managed PC-based hyperthreading CPU Windows Embedded XP real-time multi-tasking intruder detection operation system in the world Nothing moves in the Facility without being logged, recorded and, in most circumstances, terminated with extreme prejudice thanks to the banks of M18 Claymore landmines that are sewn through the Facility's acreage like contour lines on a map of the Rockies.

A man is sitting alone in a darkened section of the room. He is working the mouse of a computer and in front of him is a bank of twelve 22" flat liquid-crystal screens, the picture on each changing apparently at random. The view is somewhat monotonous, however. Although Dr Carpaccia is a nurturing person, who loves plants and gardens and especially hibiscus trees, and who loves it when neighbours pop in unannounced, she is also the sort of person who understands the need for basic security. This is why the land for a range of three miles around the Facility has been converted into a desert in which it is unsafe to walk for mines and pits with spikes at the bottom tipped with Ebola plague and HIV/AIDS and H5N1. Beyond that is a five-metre-high electrified fence. Security is also the reason Carpaccia never travels anywhere but by submarine. She is not interested in letting anyone know what type of submarine she drives, but it is expensive, anonymous and, above all, subtle.

Be that as it may, Rambouillet does not like the look of the man in front of the screens and has a word with him.

'Yo! Douche bag!' he calls. 'Show some respect, huh?'

The man looks up. He is surprised to see Dr Carpaccia in this glamourless part of the building and he jumps to his feet. He is visibly sweating and even from the door Rambouillet can smell the sickly-sweet stench of pineapple.

'Dr Capadoccia,' the man incorrectly mumbles, standing up now and bowing his head and removing his baseball cap. Dr Carpaccia is angry with him for deliberately insulting her by not using all her titles. She is, in fact, Dr Faye Carpaccia, The Presiding Genius of the Blue Ridge Mountains of Virginia, Destroyer of

Unnatural Presumption (a Dr Faye Carpaccia investigation)

The Nation's Enemies wheresoever they may be found, be it on Land or at Sea or in the Air, Summoner of Messages from beyond the Grave, Worshipped from afar by those who do not know Her and Adored by those Who Do, Queen of the Inter-Coastal Waterway, Toll Booth Owner of Interstate 64, Great High Judge of Seafood in Richmond, Cynosure of Prying Eye Wherever She goes, M.Phil, PhD, VC, CBE, ECT Etc Etc.

Dr Faye Carpaccia looks at the man and thinks that she might, if she were forced to think about it, come to despise him. She has a shortlist of people whom she appreciates more as live human beings than as dead bodies and this man is not on that list and so she resents having to share time, air and space with him. Rambouillet bundles him out of the door of the Ops room and wipes the chair that he had been sitting on clean with a pack of baby wipes that he keeps in a boot holster.

Dr Carpaccia sits down and begins to manipulate the mouse herself. Despite being fed live feeds from twelve cameras simultaneously, she finds the system easy to use and very soon they are watching the last recorded hour at the Facility. They watch each camera view at high speed with the Movement Sensor switched on. On the eighth camera the alarm pings and the images slow to reveal a man pole-vaulting over the wire fence, making sure the pole does not touch the sensors, and landing with a cat-like ease.

'Well, I'll be,' murmurs the big detective.

To begin with they think it *is* a cat, but Carpaccia zooms in and they can see that it is in fact a werewolf. I swear. A werewolf.

'My God,' mutters Carpaccia. 'It's Lou Garrooooooooooooooooo.' She ends his name with a lonesome-pine howl.

'But he is on death row in Louisiana!' exclaims Rambouillet. 'No one escapes death row in Louisiana!'

'Maybe he is on day release?' mutters Carpaccia.

She is angry and she is frightened and she is right to be angry and frightened because it was only through her tiresome work that Lou Garrew, to give him his proper name, was incarcerated on death row in Louisiana, rather than in an open prison in Virginia, because they have a zero-tolerance approach to werewolves in Louisiana and the death sentence is mandatory. And now here he was, in Virginia, weaving his way through the intricate field of landmines that her late lover, the FBI one with the strong warm tongue, had devised just before he was killed in a freak clambake accident, precisely to stop this sort of thing.

They watch as the wolf begins a high-speed zigzagging run through the minefield. Neither can believe the mines do not go off and it is as the wolf is approaching the house that it first occurs to Carpaccia that perhaps this is not Lou Garrew, but someone dressed in a werewolf costume hired from CostumeShack™.

'But the only person who knows the exact layout of the minefield is—' Rambouillet begins but stops himself.

'I know what you are going to say,' says Carpaccia. 'The only person who knows how to get through the minefield is my ex-FBI lover, the one with the strong warm tongue.'

'But he is dead!' exclaims Rambouillet.

'Or is he?' Carpaccia rhetorically asks.

They watch him now as he – whoever he is – slides open the window, left open three days earlier by someone they would now have to fire, bundle into a Bell JetRanger helicopter, fly out over the Atlantic Ocean, and drop from 1500 feet with their feet tied to the engine block of an old Hummer.

Carpaccia left clicks the mouse and they get a shot of Lou Garrew from the internal cameras. The werewolf slides quickly across the kitchen while Juanita's back is turned, opens the fridge, disappears for a second and then re-emerges, carrying a tagged bag of evidence. He exits through the window and is gone before Juanita turns round.

Carpaccia tries the other camera angles and picks him up again by the skips, towards the back of the Facility. The skips contain household rubbish and the remains of all the canvases and picture frames that Dr Carpaccia has been cutting up and destroying in her effort to prove that Beryl Cook, an octogenarian British artist, was responsible for the shot that killed JFK in Dallas. It does not surprise Dr Carpaccia that Lou Garrew heads for the skip with the trashed paintings. It merely confirms her fears that Beryl Cook is not only a werewolf but also a murderer.

As they are looking, the werewolf climbs into the skip and seems to vanish from sight. Dr Carpaccia is reaching for the phone to alert security when it rings. She exchanges another glance with Rambouillet. Carpaccia feels a fist of panic in her stomach. Only one person knows where they are.

'You answer it,' she pleadingly asks.

'I have a frog in my throat,' coughs Rambouillet.

'I'll give you five dollars to tell her I am not here,' offers Carpaccia.

'Make it ten,' counters Rambouillet.

'Done.'

Rambouillet picks up the phone.

'Hello?'

'It's me,' snaps a voice on conference call. Carpaccia flinches. It is her niece, Creepy Lesbian Niece.

'Hello, Creepy Lesbian Niece,' says Rambouillet. He is sure that Carpaccia will not want to tell her about the reappearance of the werewolf in case it brings Creepy Lesbian Niece to the Facility.

'Is my aunt there?' asks Creepy Lesbian Niece, without

greeting the detective, even though she has known him since she was ten.

'She has popped out for some milk,' bluffs Rambouillet.

'How dare you lie to me!' snaps Creepy Lesbian Niece. 'EVERYBODY knows Aunt Faye is lactose-intolerant.'

'She is getting it for Juanita,' extemporises the detective.

'Oh,' says Creepy Lesbian Niece. 'That is so like Aunt Faye. I love her! She is so kind to everybody she meets, and not just the dead ones. I am missing her so much, you bet your sweet bippy, that I am going to drive over from my townhome in Snakeskin and come and see her right this minute I am.'

Rambouillet tries to put her off. 'Oh. Well your aunt is very busy with a case right now.'

'Well,' Creepy Lesbian Niece smartly says, 'In that case she needs my help.'

'But she has all the help she needs, I promise you.'

'You are trying to deny me access to my aunt! I can tell she needs my help and that I love her more than you do!'

'That is not possible, Creepy Lesbian Niece. I love her more than anyone could, apart from that man with the warm strong tongue, and anyway that was different. And think of the dangers, Creepy Lesbian Niece! All those psychopaths and compulsive murderers out there waiting for someone in an expensive car to chase and butcher! You will never make it this far alive.'

'My love for my aunt will see me through.'

'But—'

'Butt-fuck you too!' she wittily says. 'I have devised some software that tells me when a caller is telling me untruths.'

Creepy Lesbian Niece breaks the connection.

'We have to get out of here!' Carpaccia urgently cries. 'She'll be here soon and she is so irritating that I cannot bear to be in the same room as her. Where shall we go?'

Rambouillet scratches his head, all thoughts of the stupid old werewolf forgotten now.

'What about back to Richmond? We could see what that man from Britain wants?'

4

A pair of pantyhose and a Glock pistol with Tridium sights lie bundled together on the bed of Dr Faye Carpaccia's modest Duplex and outside it the rain is falling unseasonably heavily again. The journey up from the Facility has been tense. At any moment they expected depth charges to be dropped upon them or Creepy Lesbian Niece to have developed and used some sort of submarine-crippling software, but they had parked in the underwater pen under Carpaccia's modest ranch-style Duplex in Richmond without incident and now Dr Carpaccia and Rambouillet were sitting in her office, waiting to meet the Lecturer from England.

There is a ring on the doorbell. Rambouillet unclips his holster and takes up position behind a curtain, ready for anything, while Dr Carpaccia looks through the spy hole in the middle of the door. Through the spy hole she can see four people, all dressed somewhat outlandishly. One of them is black. She cannot decide if any of them are men or women. She nods at Rambouillet who now draws his gun.

Carpaccia opens the door. She steps back, visibly shaken. All four are wearing Scotch clothes. They look crumpled and tired and in need of a wash, as if they have just come a long way by public transport. But it is not their clothes or the evidence of past perspiration that shocks Carpaccia as she looks from one to the other of the new arrivals. It is that she knows them. Or thinks she does.

There is the enormously fat African lady, for a start, who reminds her powerfully of someone she hated when she had been at that College in Britain, but then there is also the gloomy-looking man with the hang-dog face who looks as if the world will end in the next five minutes, and then there is the shifty-looking one, undernourished and maybe with rickets, with dark eyes, who has about him the mien of someone about to remove the aerial from your car. And they are all looking back at her with their mouths open, as if they recognise her. Ordinarily, she is used to this adulation and has over the years developed a way in which to deal with it, but this is different. None of these three seem remotely in awe of her, but rather confused and slightly shocked to see her, as if they had not expected her to answer her own door. They stand there and they do not know what to say, until the one whom she does not recognise, and who is slightly younger than the other three, stretches out a hand to introduce himself. Then from the corner of her eye she sees Rambouillet launch himself through the doorway, catch the hand that the younger one extends, drag the man into the house, slam him against the wall, poke the barrel of his Glock into the man's face and shout from a distance of no more than six inches that, if anyone touches Dr Faye Carpaccia, it will be him and not some pansy-assed, lily-livered, homo cock-sucking Limey in a fucking dress.

Only a massive ham-fisted blow from the black woman into the side of Rambouillet's head saves Tom Hurst from this awkward scene. It sounds like a hammer on a pumpkin. The American detective slumps to his knees, apologising to Dr Carpaccia for letting her down and straightening the lapels of Tom Hurst's jacket as he slips past, his face pressed against the Lecturer's chest, leaving a snail's trail of drool on the pleats and tucks of Tom's dress-shirt as he goes. He clutches Tom's tartan kilt before rolling to one side. Finally he lies quiet and unconscious on the parquet floor.

'Sweet smiling Baby Jesus,' says Carpaccia as Mma Ontoaste starts to laugh, a great *basso profundo* wheeze that seems to come from the bowels of the earth itself.

'Oh Mma! I have always wanted to do that.'

There is something about this woman that is monumental and it is this monumentality that appeals to Dr Carpaccia. Her skin is silky and abundant and the tartan she has picked out really matches her eyes.

'Well, I guess you had better come in,' Carpaccia politely says, standing aside to let them pass.

Mma Ontoaste is rubbing her knuckles. Tom Hurst picks up his Tam-o'-Shanter and dusts it down before putting it on his head and then taking it off again. He introduces himself and is about to introduce the others, when Rhombus saves him the trouble.

'Don't bother, Tom. We already know each other. Same year at Cuff. How are you, Faye?' he asks, stretching to kiss her cheek. 'Long time no see.'

Dr Carpaccia has never been so insulted in her life, but there is something of the charmer about this man, whom she recalls now as having been in some kind of church choir. The touch of his skin, rough with gingerish bristle, sends a charge down her spine and she wonders for a second whether his tongue is warm and strong, like the man who fell in the fire and died at the FBI summer clambake the other year.

Tom Hurst is standing stock-still. He should have expected them all to have known each other, of course, but he had not known they were in the same year. Had the Dean known when he sent Tom to see them? If not, then it cast all the clues that the murderer had been leaving in a different light. He was trying to involve the detectives. Why?

Meanwhile Rhombus is reminding Carpaccia of his name.

'Detective Inspector Scott Rhombus,' he says. 'Ex-SAS.'

'Ex-SAS, hey?' replies Carpaccia, pleased at last to shoehorn this 'joke'. 'Who do you fly with now? British Airways?'

From over Rhombus's shoulder comes a long sad noise, like the sigh of air from a lilo let down at the end of a week's vacation at the beach near Malmö.

Detective Inspector Burt Colander is laughing.

'I used to fly Virgin,' continues Carpaccia, not recognising the sound for what it is. 'But I now own a private submarine that is faster and has a further range than any other civilian submarine in existence and next year I will upgrade to an even bigger one with a further range and this one will have a full nuclear arsenal.'

There is a pause. No one quite knows what to say to this.

'But it depends on the sales of my books, I suppose,' she says, adding a curiously downbeat ending to her boast.

Rhombus walks across the spacious hallway towards the kitchen. He thinks of his own flat in Edinburgh, cold now, and able to fit easily into the kitchen of Dr Carpaccia's well-appointed but nevertheless modest townplex. A swathe of marble kitchen surface – mined in the same quarry from which the sculptor Michelangelo got his stone to sculpt his famous statue of David – reflects the thousand points of light that emit from the chandelier that Carpaccia's Creepy Lesbian Niece bought from an aristocratic French family off eBay. The appliances alone cost more than seven million dollars.

'Nice place you've got here, Faye. Always knew you'd do well.'

This is not true and Faye knows it. No one could explain her appeal then, while she had been at Cuff College, and no one can explain it now.

'You have a good sidekick,' states Colander, glancing down at Rambouillet. 'I wish I had a good sidekick.'

How he misses the simple pleasures of life in Ynstead.

The sidekick in question groans on the floor.

Anger flashes in Carpaccia's eyes. She will definitely fire Rambouillet.

'I thought Lemm Lemmingsson might be good for the role,' continues Colander, somewhat solipsistically, thinks Tom Hurst, 'but he seems a bit one-dimensional. And, whenever I go to see the new woman police officer, who is so highly thought of in Stockholm, I drink a little too much raw spirit and end up being sick in her postbox.'

Again, no one knows what to say to this. It is to be an evening of non sequiturs.

'Talking of which, Dr Carpaccia, have you anything to drink?' asks Mma Ontoaste. She has drunk heavily on the flight over, only avoiding being put off the plane in an emergency landing in Newfoundland because she fell asleep clutching a bottle of Napoleon brandy to her chest, but now her almost unquenchable thirst has returned.

After a minute they are sitting on the bar stools in the kitchen on the other side of a couple of bottles of Cabernet Sauvignon, all talking sales figures. In the microwave Carpaccia is defrosting some Turkey Twizzlers.

'What aggravates me,' she complains as she opens a jar of tomato relish she had previously bought from the 7-11, 'is that I invented the strong female character and yet no one gives me enough credit. All these silly bitches in pantyhose copying what I do make me so angry.'

Carpaccia drives the Sabatier knife she is wielding into the maple cheeseboard, neatly bisecting a piece of crackerjack cheddar on the way and sending the pieces across the table.

'You're lucky, Mma,' says Mma Ontoaste, fielding a piece of crackerjack and popping it into her mouth before anyone can blink. 'No one has ever tried to write a bargain-basement version of me. I suppose it is because I am the absolute deliberate opposite of all of you: I am a woman—'

'So am I!' Carpaccia aggressively snaps.

'So you are,' Mma Ontoaste cautiously agrees, 'but you are small and powerful and you have a massive collection of guns, not to mention your submarine—'

'What are you saying?'

'That for all your empathy with dead women, you might as well be a man,' continues Mma Ontoaste.

'Aye, owning a submarine is a wee bit phallic, is it no', Faye?'

Carpaccia is so angry she is at a loss for words. How dare this Scotch man insult her submarine? How dare this fat black woman suggest she is somehow unfeminine because she is obsessed with guns and has the phrase 'NRA4EVER' tattooed on her right buttock? Her small powerful hands and huge great big knife make quick work of chopping the Turkey Twizzlers into one-inch pieces, but she controls herself enough to put these pieces on cocktail sticks with small cubes of crackerjack and cocktail onions and pass them around.

'Go on,' she icily says. 'Help yourselves.'

'Thank you, Doctor. These are good.'

After finishing the plate, Mma Ontoaste returns to her theme.

'I am the positive print of your negatives,' she says, talking to Rhombus and Colander. 'The exact opposite to you. I am a black, tea-drinking woman with a happy marriage.'

Here Tom wonders about the state of her marriage to Mr JPS Spagatoni; wonders about the state of Mr JPS Spagatoni, if it came to that.

'I come from Botswana and see only good in things, while you are both white alcoholic males with no love in your lives, you live in the north and you see only the worst in everything.'

There is a short pause. Outside rain has begun to fall very heavily. The wind rocks the trees.

'I sometimes wonder if I deal with abstract quandaries too much,' intones Colander to no one in particular.

There is a pause. Mma Ontoaste cannot suppress a giggle and Rhombus, encouraged, starts laughing.

'Your books are shite!' he jeers.

He takes a quick sip of the wine and puts the glass heavily down on the table. The others exchange glances. Tom Hurst opens his mouth to speak, but Rhombus continues.

'I'll say this for you, though, pal: you've managed to make a career out of nothing. And I mean nothing. Nothing ever happens in Sweden. There is no crime at all. You invent the crimes and then go around suggesting they have some wider implication.'

Mma Ontoaste jumps to Colander's defence.

'Well, Rra, your books deal with the same sorts of things, don't they? Corruption in the police force; the rich, the poor; escaping the past; the SAS; and then something topical like immigration or cannibalism.'

Cannibalism? thinks Rhombus. He wonders how many of his books she has read.

'Er, look,' says Tom Hurst, trying to calm things down. 'Let's agree that any of our perceived faults as writers are more to do with the limitations of the Genre and the human desire for strong stories, however improbable either may be and then let's leave it at that, shall we?'

A vague truce is called.

'Okay, let's all drink to huge sales figures and forget about it.'

Carpaccia opens a bottle of vintage Cristal champagne but she will not offer any of the champagne to Rhombus until he apologises to her submarine. Nor does she offer any to Mma Ontoaste until she admits it is perfectly natural to own something like a thousand guns.

'Including three 50-calibre machine guns?' she asks.

'Including three 50-calibre machine guns,' agrees Mma Ontoaste.

'Can we talk about why we are here?' asks Tom. He explains about the death of Claire Morgan.

'Oh, the poor thing!' exclaims Carpaccia. 'I feel for her already. Did you bring the body? I bet she is covered in some kind of coppery residue.'

'It's possible,' he agrees, before explaining the series of clues that have brought them to Virginia. As Tom continues, the brevity of his case becomes apparent. When he is finished there is silence for a while until Mma Ontoaste snores suddenly.

'I think you are being played with,' suggests Carpaccia. 'Often what happens in my cases is that I discover all this weird stuff about the dead bodies that have absolutely nothing to do with how I catch the criminal in the end.'

Carpaccia is not used to drink and is becoming confessional.

'Mostly it's chance,' she continues. 'Sometimes something I find out about the body does help catch the criminal, but there are times when I wonder why anyone lets me near the criminal investigative process.'

'I'm like that,' Rhombus impatiently agrees. 'Especially as I am usually suspended or "in the frame" for the murder in the first place.'

'I usually get a pretty clear idea who the murderer is,' enjoins Colander, 'and then I get into my tracksuit and take a gun into the woods and sort of roll about in the pine needles and mud until the murderer turns up and then I shoot him.'

'Oh, yes. Luck plays a big part,' agrees Mma Ontoaste. 'No doubt about it.'

There is a silence for a while. Sips of drink are taken, Twizzlers eaten.

'What sort of stroke of luck are you hoping for in this case, Tom?' Colander dolefully asks after a while. Tom does not really know.

'I suppose I was hoping you would come up with something. You seem to be the luckiest detectives alive.'

'Amen to that,' agrees Rhombus. 'Hey! I wonder what happened to the others in our year at Cuff. Do any of you see anyone from those days?'

There is a round of regretful head-shaking.

'I wonder what happened to that old guy who solved crimes while stacking shelves at a DIY store somewhere in middle England?'

'He wore an orange tabard, didn't he? With a slogan that said something like "stop me if you need any help".'

'I bet he's still there.'

'It's good to have a trade, Rra,' muses Mma Ontoaste. 'That way you have something in the quiet times.'

'And wasn't there an Eskimo? What was his name?'

'I remember him, Rra! His name was Nak-ka-khoo. He tried to kiss me once.'

'God, yes. Now he was really stupid. How did he ever get a

place at College at all? He couldn't detect his way out of a paper bag, could he? He was always failing his practicals.'

'And he could hardly string a sentence together.'

There is an embarrassed silence for a second.

'But couldn't he hypnotise people?'

'And he was a musician. He could play loads of musical instruments. He could play the viola, the viola. Like the Music Man.'

Dr Carpaccia stretches across to jot down the name of her next compulsive murderer: the Music Man.

'Oh Rra, he used to play the most wonderful music. He played the Spanish guitar and all the girls would . . .' She stopped and took a sip of her wine.

'Anyway,' she said. 'It was a long time ago.'

'The strange thing is that I think I saw him the other day,' murmurs Colander.

'You saw Nak-ka-khoo? How odd. Where?'

'He was – wait, let me think. He was in a shop somewhere. Buying something. Yes, he was buying something in a shop, but what?'

'And where? In Ynstead?' asks Tom urgently.

'I think so, but it could have been Malmö. Wait a second it was in Malmö. At the video store. He was renting a video. I thought at the time that it was him, but I was in a real hurry and I could not be sure and then it hit me only later.'

'What does he look like now?'

'The same,' shrugs Colander. 'Small; dark hair; weather-beaten face; fishing pole; fur-lined hood; shoulders hunched from all that fishing.'

'Oh, Rra! That is strange. That sounds exactly like my new assistant, Mma Murakami. She locked herself in her office all day and I hardly saw her, but she looked just like that.'

'Did you ever see her handle a canoe?' Carpaccia sharply asks.

'No. But she did play jazz on her radio, and she smelled strongly of fish, now that I come to think of it.'

'Fish?'

'And seal meat and whale blubber, I suppose.'

'And jazz? That is odd. The new officer from Stockholm who was called Knut Knutsson was always playing jazz on his radio in the next-door office.'

Rhombus is looking worried.

'I heard some music in a kitchen in Edinburgh that made me forget for a second who I was or what I was supposed to be doing too. Ah. A haunting refrain; the power of cheap music.'

'And those notebooks!' recalls Tom Hurst. 'Sealskin.'

'How strange. We have been finding bodies in Florida bound in fishing twine.'

The weight of coincidence reaches a tipping point.

'All right,' says Tom Hurst. 'I am ringing the Dean to see if I can find out where Nak-ka-khoo is now.'

None of the detectives look convinced.

'But it could be anyone,' says Rhombus. 'I mean have you no' walked down the street, heard some music playing – some Eric Clapton, for example – and you just start tapping your feet and, before you know it, a whole afternoon has passed?'

'And just because I thought I saw him doesn't mean anything.'

'And my assistant looking a little like someone Burt thought he saw? Rra, I know he could be good at disguises but Nak-ka-khoo and I "knew" each other at Cuff. I do not think that Mma Murakami could be Nak-ka-khoo in disguise.'

'And the fact that someone is tying chickens up with fishing twine? C'mon. It's too far-fetched.'

It struck Tom then just how far these detectives were off-song.

He had fought them all the way to Richmond, reminding them to trust their instincts, to seize on one particular thing and go with that, just as they had learned in the first year at Cuff, but now here they were ignoring the most fantastically oblique chain of clues in favour of rational observations and, God forbid, Probability.

Before he can say anything, they are dazzled by star-bright white light shining in through the Venetian blinds at all the kitchen windows. The detectives flinch and try to cover their eyes. All are panicked.

'What is it?' asks Mma Ontoaste, her voice rising maybe a couple of octaves.

'Put your weapons down and your hands up!' blares an amplified voice from the darkness outside the house. 'Come on out, Aunty Faye! I have the house surrounded. There is no escape.'

'Oh, sweet smiling Baby Jesus!' Carpaccia whispers. 'I recognise that voice! It's Creepy Lesbian Niece! Get down, everybody. There is no telling what she will do.'

They slide off their chairs, copying Carpaccia, and onto their hands and knees. They are staring wildly at one another now.

'What does she want?' Tom asks.

'It's you I want, Aunty Faye,' comes the booming voice again. 'I know everybody else loves you the most but I love you even more than that and I mean to make you mine and mine alone!'

'Quick!' Carpaccia whispers. 'To the submarine!'

There is a chaotic scramble back through Carpaccia's house as behind them there is a deafening explosion. Creepy Lesbian Niece has bazooka-ed the kitchen in which minutes ago they had been having a quiet drink. The noise is awful. The blast is fearsome. Scraps of metal and wood fly down the corridor after the fleeing detectives, followed by a rolling cloud of choking dust and smoke.

'Well, butter my biscuit!' Carpaccia exclaims. 'That ungrateful bitch!'

In the hallway she turns and opens a door from which steps lead down to her indoor submarine pen, where the green water softly laps against cinderblock walls. Moored in the middle is a small M8-63 hi-tech submarine made in Norway and usually used in off-shore salvage operations. It is slate-grey and barnacled in places. The hatch to the conning tower stands open.

'Quick!' Carpaccia urges. 'The gangway.'

She gestures with the barrel of a Tokyo Marui M4 R.I.S. automatic rifle that has appeared as if from nowhere and the four detectives run as fast as they are able down the stairs and along the dock, their footsteps ringing loud on the steel mesh beneath them.

'Nice murals,' says Rhombus, admiring the marbled walls that line the pen.

It is a struggle to get Mma Ontoaste into the submarine but with some pushing she is soon past the hatches and down the ladder, where she and all the others are bathed in the green glow of the submarine's navigation system.

'Thank God for cocoa butter,' Mma Ontoaste says, rolling her black dress down her thighs.

Carpaccia follows them down the ladder, sealing the conning hatch above her head and dropping down into the galley. There is not much room for manoeuvre but she squeezes past the detectives and seats herself in the captain's chair.

'There's no reasoning with her when she is in that mood,' Carpaccia, referring to her niece, says. 'We just have to give her time and space and hope to hell she has not invented some damned software that will take us off course.'

Through a porthole they can see only the black water of the tunnel that Carpaccia tells them will lead them to the James River and from there to wherever they need to go. Carpaccia types some coordinates into an onboard computer and beneath their feet a turbine whirrs and the submarine sinks and jerks forward. They are off.

'Where are we going?' asks Rhombus. 'Back to Scotland?'

'We need to find Nak-ka-khoo,' urges Tom.

'He could be anywhere, Tom. We do not know where he is and we do not know where to start. Any start we do make might be in the wrong direction. I am not convinced we will ever find him. In fact, I do not see how we might ever find him.'

'But I think he wants to be found,' counters Tom. There is a pause. Colander does not know what to say.

'You are good at this, you know, Rra. For a second I believed you and I am beginning to think we ought to find him.'

'I need to call the Dean or Professor Wikipedia,' says Tom.

'Too dangerous,' says Captain Carpaccia. 'We can only make calls when the periscope is up. There is a lot of shipping in the canal and Creepy Lesbian Niece will be on the lookout. There is no telling what she might do if she sees us.'

'Damn that Creepy Lesbian Niece,' mutters Rhombus. 'Without my SAS skills we would have been dead in there.'

'Uh, Mma Ontoaste?' Carpaccia kindly interrupts, her slate-blue eyes glancing up from the screen. 'Could you sit down towards the back? You are affecting the ballast.'

They can hear water thronging beyond the thin riveted skin as the submarine speeds on down the tunnel and into the James River. Condensation gathers. There is silence in the cabin. No one is comfortable now, least of all Mma Ontoaste, who is squeezed into the back, sitting on a gunny sack and a half a hundredweight of mung beans. After half an hour Carpaccia types a new command into the system and the submarine begins to rise to the surface.

The water around them begins to clear and they can see the light on the surface above.

'Periscope up,' she crisply snaps, pressing a button and swivelling in her chair to intercept two handles as the polished body of the periscope rises from the deck. She snaps down some handles and peers through the eyepieces, left, right, scanning the shipping and the shore.

'All clear,' she says. 'You can make your call now. It should work.'

Tom dials the number on his cell phone. The phone in far-off Oxford rings a few times before it is picked up. Tom recognises the voice instantly. Alice Appleton. He has not spoken to Alice since she fainted in the Library.

'Hello, Tom,' she begins. 'Long time no see. Where are you? You sound like you are at the bottom of the ocean.'

She is friendly but off-hand and explains that the Dean is on a fund-raising drive, but she is not sure where. This is common, of course. Tom explains what he is after.

'Nak-ka-khoo?' she says. 'I've never heard of it.'

'It's a "he". He was in the year of '74 at Cuff.'

'I thought I knew of everyone still alive who had been to Cuff – even that one who solved mysteries in DIY superstores and the trout farmer from Ecuador. I'll have to check the Library. I'll call you back.'

When he disconnects the phone the detectives are looking at him speculatively.

'So the Dean isn't there?'

'No. He's trying to raise funds for a memorial statue to Claire Morgan.'

'Funny sort of detail to include,' Rhombus snorts.

'Do you think it might be important?' asks Tom.

'I feel sick,' wails Mma Ontoaste from the back of the submarine. They are moving at 25 knots down the James River now, pitching and yawing as they approach the city Newport News and the ocean.

Tom's cell-phone rings. It is Alice Appleton.

'I've found him,' she says. 'His last address was a poste restante in a town called Pond Inlet, in Canada. He's become a meteorologist.'

'So—?'

'So he's done nothing. Never written a word. Never solved a case. There just is no crime up there because there are no people up there.'

'Sounds like Sweden,' Rhombus darkly mutters, but the detectives look at one another significantly. The frustration would be unbearable. If there was no crime to solve, a detective often turned to committing it.

'You said that that was his last address?'

'Yes. Last year we sent him an invite to next week's Gaudy Night.'

'And?'

'And he's down here as coming.'

'When is the Gaudy Night?' Tom asks.

'In three days' time.'

'Okay. We'll be back.'

'We?'

'All of us – Mma Ontoaste, Inspectors Colander and Rhombus and Dr Carpaccia.'

'Oh, not that poison dwa—'

Tom terminates the call and grins fixedly at Dr Carpaccia.

'Don't say we are going to have to get there by submarine,' groans Mma Ontoaste.

'A private plane might have been a better choice,' admits Carpaccia sadly, lowering the periscope and preparing the onboard computer to dive.

'Chart a course for Oxford, England.'

Part VI

Another Gaudy Night

1

A conversation by the fire . . .

'Well,' said the Dean, raising a glass of champagne to Professor Wikipedia. 'Here's to fund-raising.'

'Indeed,' replied Wikipedia, raising his own flute, a twinkle in his eye. 'The process of soliciting money by requesting donations from individuals, businesses, charitable foundations or governmental agencies!'

They were both wearing dinner jackets, standing by the hissing fire in the Dean's study, their academic gowns on coat-hangers hooked over the picture rail. It was seven o'clock in the evening and the alumni of Cuff College had gathered in town to celebrate Gaudy Night. About now, all over town, they would be squeezing their prosperous middle-aged bodies into evening clothes and wondering how one another would look. In an hour the Dean was due in the Junior Common Room to welcome them with more champagne and the first of his speeches imploring generosity.

'I used to hate the Gaudy,' he said. 'All those smug bloody alumni coming back and looking at you as if you've somehow aged more than they have. Looking at you as if you've achieved nothing in life.'

Wikipedia disagreed.

'I've always found crime writers to be rather understanding.

Some of them are even envious of us, you know, quietly eking out our allotted span in this quiet spot, while they are at the mercies of the vagaries of market forces and literary whim.'

'Fashions do change,' agreed the Dean. 'And it is true some of them are up one day, down the next, but I always feel they are looking at me as if I don't really know what it's like.'

'And now you do,' smiled Wikipedia. 'Congratulations are in order.'

Once more glasses were raised and eyes were met.

'We'll see,' said the Dean. 'To be honest, I am just glad he's back.'

'He must have had a rough time?' asked Wikipedia. 'Being a meteorologist is no fun, I imagine, especially on – Baffin Island was it?'

'A place called Pond Inlet,' nodded the Dean, pulling a face as if he wished he could unsay something just said.

'Ah. Pond Inlet,' Wikipedia said, warming to his subject. 'A small, predominantly Inuit community in Nunavut located at the top of Baffin Island, with a population of more than 1200 people, the largest of the four hamlets above the 72nd parallel in Canada.'

'That's the one, but please,' said the Dean holding up a hand. 'I never want to hear another word about Pond Inlet ever again. I don't know why I sent him there in the first place. I just thought it was time for something different from an English village or one of these bloody colleges.'

'But it was a good idea, wasn't it? An isolated and enclosed community. Lots of atmosphere. Dark at night. Well, in fact dark for very nearly six months of the year.'

'Yes, but there was simply nothing bad to do except drink too much home-made alcohol and shoot polar bears. I wanted him to be able to solve crimes with reference to snowboot size and that sort of thing. Like Miss Smilla.'

'Oh, Miss Smilla. Is she coming tonight?'

The Dean shook his head.

'To be honest, I've never quite been able to forgive her for that strange sex stuff in the bathroom.'

'Oh yes. When she—'

'That's the one,' interrupted the Dean. 'I suppose I should have invited her. She and Nak-ka-khoo could have talked about their feeling for snow.'

'But his feeling for it is rather bad, isn't it?'

'Yes. To tell you the truth, I've been a bit worried about him. It seems all those years have made him a bit . . .'

The Dean shrugged and took a sip of his champagne.

'Dark?' Wikipedia suggested.

'Yes. I suppose that's it.'

'In Western tradition darkness is associated with evil, or evil entities, such as demons or Satan, as well as Hell or, especially in Egyptian mythology, the underworld.'

'Yes.'

'It's a concept personified in the character of Darkness played by Tim Curry in a 1985 fantasy film called *Legend*, wherein Darkness took the form of a fifteen-foot-high stereotype of Satan, complete with reddened skin, long horns and cloven hooves.'

The slightest drawing together of those famous eyebrows suggested that the Dean had had just about enough of this sort of thing from Wikipedia.

'You know, Professor,' he began, 'sometimes what begins as a character's harmless little quirk can, over the pages of a novel, turn into something really very irritating.'

Wikipedia looked hurt.

'You're surely not referring to me?'

'No, no. Of course not,' the Dean said quickly, pouring Wikipedia another couple of inches of champagne. 'It's Nak-ka-khoo and his endless practical jokes. Ransacking Tom's study like that and then giving him that fright. There's something vengeful about it.'

'Well, it's hardly surprising,' Wikipedia said, resisting for once the temptation to define. 'I'd turn bad up there. Still, bringing him down here to murder Claire was genius. A real stroke of genius.'

'To tell you the truth, Aldous, and this is strictly *entre nous*, it wasn't entirely my idea. He'd joined a circus, you know? The one that sets up on Headington Hill. It's where he learned to do all that acrobatic stuff he does. He was supposed to be taking care of the seals, you know, with pilchards and spinning balls and so forth, but he'd become so used to culling the damned things in Canada that – well, it didn't go according to plan. He wanted to be a snake charmer, you know? But they said there was no call and they threw him out. He turned up here, out of the blue, as it were, without a penny in his pocket.'

'My God. And whose idea was it get all the others involved?'

'Ontoaste and so forth? A bit of both, to tell you the truth. I could see it would take years of churning out a novel a year for him to get anywhere and he just hasn't got the patience, the poor thing, and so I was casting around for something really special. He spent all day brooding about his time here – about how successful the others had become. He began carving little voodoo dolls.'

'Ah! Voodoo, or Vodun in Benin, the term applied to the branches of a West African ancestor-based spiritist-animist religious tradition that—'

'Yes, that. Eventually I decided I'd better get him out of here. Well, he wouldn't go back to Pond Inlet and you know I always like to get away at Christmas so, while I was looking for cheap flights, the idea occurred to me: why not use my contacts? Take him with me. The idea snowballed from there. You know – he has some pretty unique talents? We had quite a trip – Botswana, Sweden, Edinburgh, of course, for New Year, and then Virginia, and then – well, we've got all sorts of plans for the future.'

'Your travel agent must have been delighted.'

'Yes, it took some doing. Said I'd mention him – a chap called Tony at TrailFinders on Kensington High Street – if anything came of it.'

Wikipedia raised his glass again.

'You're a genius, Dean, an absolute genius.'

'Not at all, Aldous, not at all. Besides, I could never have done it without you. All that information about that spear got Tom Hurst on his way.'

'Nevertheless, Dean. Chapeaux. Chapeaux.'

'Well, you are too kind, Aldous, old boy, but now I had better be off. They'll start arriving soon and I want to make sure that Nak-ka-khoo is ready.'

They unhooked their gowns from the hangers and left each other in the Winter Gardens. The Dean walked briskly across the New Quad to a door in the corner, watched by a puzzled-looking Wikipedia. It was going to be a beautiful, if cold, night and the Dean could see the stars were out already. He opened the door and began the long climb up to Nak-ka-khoo's bedroom on the fifth floor.

He was trying to think when he had ever felt more pleased with the way things were going. Wikipedia was right. He was brilliant. When he had first created Nak-ka-khoo, all those years ago now, he had been slightly too *avant garde* for his time, he could see that now. Out of place among all the procedurals and, of course, very foreign. Putting the boy through Cuff College had cost him dear and the long years afterwards, when no publisher in the land, not even Canongate, had been even slightly interested, had been dispiriting. Now though, now that he had brought Nak-ka-khoo down from that Godforsaken island and had him leave all those bafflingly inane clues all round the world so that Tom Hurst and those swollen-headed morons would stumble upon them, now that he had done that, the Dean was being bombarded with offers from every cash-rich publisher in the land. Six figures! And all that bloody respect he would earn.

He allowed himself a long peal of laughter that echoed across the New Quad, all the way to the New Library, where Alice Appleton sat with her head bowed over a book. The air around her still smelled of damp wood where she had scrubbed at the stains of Claire Morgan's blood. She looked up and shivered. It had sounded like a hyena.

2

Landfall . . .

On the River Thames between London and Oxford there are no fewer than 32 locks, and piloting a submarine through each of them is not easy, even with the help of the obliging lock-keepers. It had taken Captain Carpaccia and the four detectives just three days to cross the Atlantic, following the Gulf Stream all the way from Richmond, Virginia, in the USA, to Land's End in England, but now, as they powered their way up the Thames past Sonning, it looked like they might be late for the Gaudy.

It had been a fraught journey. Just as they had crossed the Laurentian Abyss in the North Atlantic Ocean, Captain Carpaccia explained that Creepy Lesbian Niece was incapable of letting her go, and while the submarine they were travelling in was a hi-spec super-sub, capable of 100 knots an hour, Creepy Lesbian Niece had a hi-hi-spec super-super-sub, capable of even higher speeds.

'And hers is panelled in cherry wood, inside and out.'

This unwelcome news had haunted the crew all the way to the point where the Thames becomes the Cherwell, but by then Carpaccia had whipped all but Mma Ontoaste into shape and by the time they rose out of the turgid waters at Magdalen Bridge, morale was high.

'Oh, Rra,' said Mma Ontoaste, addressing Tom. 'It has come

back to where it all began. Imagine how much time and money you would have saved by being paraplegic and unable to travel.'

'Or if you had been eight months pregnant,' suggested Rhombus.

'Or in an iron lung.'

'Or a coffin.'

Despite the time that had passed since he had learned that Nakka-khoo had murdered Claire Morgan, Tom was still not yet in the mood for this sort of banter. He was exhausted from the effort of keeping the detectives apart and had come to the point where he did not really care for them or the case or, in fact, anything very much. He was in the grip of black nihilist rage. He could see that from the very outset he had been played with, and that perhaps a more experienced detective, or a disabled one, or a pregnant one, or even a dead one, might not have so enthusiastically pursued all the conclusions to which he had jumped.

He wondered if he ought to have kept notes on what had happened. After all, this was something that he could write up and turn if not into a bestseller, then into something at least. He studied his companions again, wondering what made them so special.

There was Mma Ontoaste, with apparently limitless reserves of compassion, bush tea and cocoa butter, as well as those cursed Botswana skies, of course, but now, after a few days under water, she looked sunken and depleted. She had not had a drink in days and had lost kilos. She had reacted the worst to their sub-aquatic confinement and had been snappish and ill-tempered ever since Captain Carpaccia had rationed her to one piece of toast at breakfast.

Meanwhile, Colander was happy doing logic problems from a back copy of *The Puzzler* magazine, wetting the tip of a blunted navigation pencil and filling in the answers without any trace of the hesitancy and morbid self-doubt that usually characterised his investigations. He too had lost weight and was even whistling a happy tune.

DI Rhombus, being a Scot, was used to the lack of sun and the cramped and noisome conditions. He had kept himself busy trying to recall all the goals scored by (or, more trickily, against) the Scotch national football side in World Cup competitions. With no privacy on the sub, he had been unable to Dwell on his Time in the SAS and, although he had tried to suggest that crime writers were really frustrated rock stars, Tom had only had to mention PD James to stop him taking that line too far.

And if Captain Carpaccia had been strangely muted and thoughtful, Tom put it down to the responsibility she had shouldered as captain of the *SS Stalker*. It occurred to him that perhaps she would be happier being the captain of a pleasure cruiser or maybe the unelected head, or fuehrer even, of a small but mightily well-armed boutique nation-state, rather than an implausibly tetchy mortician with an inquisitive streak.

'Stand by,' ordered Carpaccia as they approached the wharf by Magdalen Bridge, deserted now, with the punts neatly stored for the winter.

'DI Rhombus, throw a line, will you?'

'A line? You mean a joke?'

'Rope. Tie a rope onto a bollard so we can tie up.'

Rope. Old rope. It was then that it really struck Tom. That was their genius: their ability to recycle rope. It was the same old rope every time, wasn't it? Braided and plaited, bound and knotted in subtly different ways, but ultimately always the same piece of rope, the same personal piece of rope that they had started with, uncoiled, re-coiled, twisted and woven in different ways. It was this secret, this shared knowledge, that gave them all this grumbling pleasure in each other's company.

The submarine docked with a gentle bump and Colander, first out of the hatch, lowered the gangway from the conning tower and held it steady as Mma Ontoaste led them onto dry land. It was dark and the air crisp and almost too sharp to breathe after the fug of the submarine. For a moment they looked like five drunks, staggering along Musgrave Street, too hurried to take the time to let their sea legs acclimatise to the dry land. Ahead of them were the *flambeaux* in sconces in the wall of the façade of Cuff College, lit to celebrate the Gaudy.

'My God, it has hardly changed at all!' puffed Colander. 'Or perhaps it is we who have not changed?'

Tom could almost hear Rhombus rolling his eyes at this remark. The two men had bickered on the trip over, but had never come to blows – possibly because Mma Ontoaste had withdrawn her favours from both and slept in her own chaste berth next to Captain Carpaccia. Mma Ontoaste was used to solving such awkward problems.

The porter stepped from his lodge to say something to them as they crossed Sjuzet Bridge, where, it seemed years ago now, Tom had stopped to finish his cigarette.

'What's all this, then?' he started, but stopped and stared open-mouthed. It occurred to Tom only then that although they had grown used to the sight of one another, to others they might look unusual. With the exception of Carpaccia – who was wearing a full naval outfit in keeping with her rank as captain of a submarine – they were still in full Highland fig and looked terribly drunk.

Carpaccia had been half expecting the porters to stop her and throw her out of the College, as they had done all those years before over the missing adverbs and the case of the misunderstood thesaurus, and so she had her trusty Tokyo Marui M4 R.I.S. automatic rifle at the ready. The porter stepped back into the warmth of his lodge and let the door shut quietly behind him.

3

Unexpected guests . . .

The Dining Hall of Cuff College is a splendid room, longer than it is wide, with a high, ribbed ceiling from which chandeliers hang on long chains. The walls are punctuated with heavy oil portraits in baroque frames and the dark wood panelling is etched with faded gold letters to mark long-since-forgotten academic or sporting success. At one end of the room, under a stained-glass window that shows Cain murdering Abel, a high table is raised on a dais. Below this are two further tables, each more than 30 foot long, filled that night with the brightest and the best in detective fiction, including most of the Americans who had come over on scholarships, the Swedes and all the other more marginal characters at work in the Genre today. The din of conversation and chink of china and cutlery was constant. Waiters darted up and down the lines of men and women, all in their finest, serving what was roundly agreed to be execrable food and indifferent wine.

The Dean sat at the top table, with a very large female police commissioner from Manchester on one hand and a glamorous forensic scientist from Montreal on the other. He was laughing at a joke he had made and taking compliments on the very fine speech he had just delivered in the Junior Common Room.

'So, Dean,' purred the forensic scientist whose name – something like Tempura (but no one would be named after a type of batter, surely?) – the Dean could not get the hang of. 'Where is the hero of the hour?'

'Ah! Nak-ka-khoo? He is over there. Talking to a publisher.'

They studied the scene. Nak-ka-khoo did not look like a terribly graceful dinner companion: he was a stranger to conversation and he had spent long enough in the tundra to know that you eat when there is food, starve when there is none, and so he was forcing food and wine into his mouth, his eyes all the while resolutely bolted to the cleavage of the dark-haired woman sitting on the opposite side of the table. Nak-ka-khoo was a wolfish-looking man, with long dark hair and a sallow, closed face. His body was somehow ill-suited to the constraints of a bow-tie and dinner shirt.

'Oh, he looks charming,' murmured the woman, not for a second meaning it. 'I hear he can skin a polar bear in less than a minute?'

'Yes. It is just one of his party pieces,' the Dean agreed. 'He is also a talented snake charmer. He can do it with just an ocarina and a dab of Vaseline.'

'But he can't speak English?'

'Not very well,' admitted the Dean with a sigh. 'That has held him back, I must say, and made him rather frustrated.'

The Dean had hoped any Nak-ka-khoo adventures would be translated into English, of course, but he had timed it badly; just as soon as there was an appetite for foreign detective fiction among general readers, the Crime Writers' Association had barred translations from their awards. The Dean would now have to teach Nak-ka-khoo English if he was ever to get the Golden Dagger he so coveted.

The Dean took a sip of his wine and speared a slice of watery courgette on his fork. Further down the table was Alice Appleton, looking, the Dean thought, very fetching in some dark-blue dress that showed off her shoulders and what he could only think of as her upper chest. She was listening to Wikipedia banging on about something.

'A chicken can be hypnotised too, you know,' he was saying, his mind obviously very much on Nak-ka-khoo. 'By holding its head down and continuously drawing a line along the ground with a stick, starting at its beak and extending straight outwards in front. It'll remain immobile for anywhere between 15 seconds to 30 minutes, continuing to stare at the line.'

'Really?' asked Alice, genuinely interested. 'How on earth did they discover that?'

'Well, the first known reference to it was in 1646, in *Mirabile Experimentum de Imaginatione Gallinae* by a man called Athanasius Kircher, but how he found out about it – well, I suppose one might have to read his book, but you know – who can be bothered? Hello. What's this?'

At that moment Tom Hurst and the other detectives came through the door at the other end of the room. They stood in an untidy group.

'It's Tom!' cried Alice, flushing slightly. 'He made it.'

The top table went quiet. The Dean stood up, his pale face clenched, his eyebrows drawn. His eyes flicked from Tom and the detectives to Nak-ka-khoo. Conversation and hubbub at the tables petered out until there was silence. The Dean had no need to tap his glass to attract attention, but did so anyway.

'Ladies and gentlemen,' he began. 'I can't tell you how glad I am that tonight we have with us, by some amazing feat of navigation, not to mention—' and here the Dean was genuinely lost for words '—all the other things, none other than four of our most successful alumni from, I think, the class of '74.'

He introduced the detectives and there was a ripple of respectful applause. Tom Hurst led them between the tables until they reached the top table.

'Dean,' began Tom, 'I know who killed Claire Morgan.'

There was a gasp of taken breath all around him. Claire Morgan's murder had been on everybody's lips.

'Oh yes, dear Claire. So much missed. But surely this can wait until tomorrow, Tom? Don't want to cast a shadow over the Gaudy, do we? Why don't you all sit down? Have a drink.'

'I should say that the murderer is in this room.'

There was another collective gasp. Nak-ka-khoo, unable to understand English, had no idea what was going on and was yet to appreciate just who the detectives were or what they were saying. He was forcing a chicken breast down his mouth.

'He sure is, Dean,' Carpaccia started, jumping in front of Tom, swinging her rifle about carelessly. 'When I was examining the bodies of the chickens so senselessly slaughtered in Florida, I noticed a powdery residue that glittered coppery under Electron Microscopy. It turned out to be resident in a particular brand of talcum powder that you can only buy on the internet. By getting Creepy Lesbian Niece to hack into the internet company's records, I discovered that the talcum powder is regularly ordered by a man who has the Canadian hand-made moccasin slipper franchise. Now his slippers are made from the pelt of a particular kind of beaver that only lives north of latitude 66° 33' 39'—'

Wikipedia jumped to his feet to say something.

'Not now, Aldous, really,' snapped the Dean. 'Mma Ontoaste, you seem the most sensible. What on earth is going on here?'

But Mma Ontoaste was not listening to the Dean. She had left their party and approached one of the long tables, where she dragged a small man in a slightly shabby dinner jacket to his feet and was shaking his hand with such enthusiasm it was as if she meant to yank it off.

'Clovis Andersen,' she was laughing. 'How I love your book!'

Clovis Andersen was blinking nervously and his face was gripped in a glassy smile. He could not get away.

'But, Dean,' continued Rhombus, 'I discovered a piece of paper that described ritualistic killings of ptarmigan by men who wore tweed plus-fours and had all been at school with one another. On the back of it, in tiny letters, was the name of the Scotch Minister for Canadian Affairs, written in blue-black ink, the same sort of ink that they use on the release forms at HMP Barlinnie. I had DS Shortbread poke about a bit, because I couldn't do it myself, on account of being in the frame, and I discovered that a thriving rat run exists, involving Canadian giant squid ink, chip suppers and NAZI GOLD, but that's not all—'

Then it was Colander's turn to butt in.

'Don't listen to the officer from Scotchland, Dean, or the pseudo-forensic scientist from Richmond, Virginia. Neither of them know what they are talking about. I am not sure I am taking this investigation the right way here either. It could be anything. Let's be honest, none of us really know anything. Perhaps we should call a meeting? Can I have a cup of coffee? In fact, I don't like the look of him. I bet he is a threat to our children. I am going to slip into my tracksuit now and shoot him in the head until he is quite dead.'

'Hold me back someone, or I'll kill the Swedish bastard!' bellowed Rhombus. No one moved to restrain him.

Colander blinked.

'Everyone knows you are secretly Welsh,' he said, and that was enough. Rhombus leapt at Colander, his arms outstretched, hoping, it seemed, to tear him apart. Even from where Tom was standing, this did not look like the sort of tactic that the SAS might teach anyone. There was some pushing and shoving. Both men were red-faced, flapping and slapping at each other and springing in the air like some modern dance routine. Rhombus took a kick at Colander, catching him on the knee. Colander squealed and ran at Rhombus, catching him off balance and crashing back into the table behind. The women screamed and scrambled aside, the men fending the writhing bodies off with stiff arms.

'Tom! Stop them!' Alice cried. Tom didn't know where to begin. He pulled Rhombus's Tam-o'-Shanter off his head and slapped him with it, but the men were too intent on the fight. Meanwhile the Dean had caught Nak-ka-khoo's eye and the Eskimo was pushing his chair back, having finally understood the need to get away.

'Now! Grip my grits, you two stop that wrestlin', you hear?' cried Carpaccia, swinging the machine gun round and pointing it at the ceiling. She let loose a quick burst of gunfire that had two immediate effects. The first was to stop the fight instantly, but the second was to snap a link in the chain that held the chandeliers in place. There was a staccato rattling above their heads as the chain flew through the eyes holding it in place and the chandelier dropped sharply to catch the fleeing Nak-ka-khoo a sharp and, as it later turned out, fatal, blow on the head. He staggered a step and then crumpled headlong across the table as the rest of the long chain came crashing down, covering him in heavy links of antique iron.

'Nak-ka-khoo!' cried the Dean, enraged with pain. He ran and hauled the chain off the young man's body and was in time to feel Nak-ka-khoo's last breath before he died.

'Now look at what you've done, you bloody fool,' he snapped

at Carpaccia. 'You've killed him! Killed off the best detective in the land, a man who learned the art of snake charming at the feet of the great Baba Gulabgir—'

'Ah,' started Wikipedia. 'Baba Gulabgir, or Gulabgarnath, became the Guru of snake charmers; legendarily teaching his disciples to revere snakes, not fear them as they—'

'Aldous,' cried the Dean. 'For the love of God, will you for once just SHUT UP?'

'But, Rra,' intoned Mma Ontoaste. 'A great detective does not need to do all those things. A great detective needs only intuition and a few very simple problems that anyone with any sense could sort out in seconds.'

'Oh, Christ! I've just about had enough of your horseshit.'

It was not a wise thing to say. Mma Ontoaste caught him by the hair at the side of his head and lifted him so that he was dancing on tiptoes.

'Call the police,' he yelped.

'Surely not before we find out why he killed Claire, though?' asked Rhombus, wiping a bloody lip from the fight. 'I mean, *I* know why he killed her, of course, but for dramatic effect and all these people will want to know.'

He pointed at the guests, managing to include in his gesture Colander, who looked like he might attack him again at any moment. The guests knew the form detective fiction is supposed to take and there were nods all round, and even the Dean agreed that some kind of explanation was necessary.

'I'll tell you,' panted the Dean. 'Just so long as you put me down and that fucker over there – Aldous fucking Wiki-fucking-pedia – doesn't interrupt.'

Aldous promised. Or pledged, rather.

'It was foolproof,' began the Dean. 'A simple plan to eliminate the opposition. Nothing illegal about that. I was going to get enough clues together so that Tom here would round up every detective working in the Genre today and have them working on the same silly case. By the end of it there would be a band of 30 or 40 of you travelling by bus all over the world. Meanwhile Nak-ka-khoo would clean up in the vacuum. All your crazy serial killers, compulsive bed-wetting murderers, lunatic flesh-eating mummy's boys, stalker vampires and werewolves would have been his to catch. I had a deal! A publishing deal!'

The Dean dropped next to the dead body of Nak-ka-khoo and hammered his fists on the ground, his body wracked by sobs. Sobs for what might once have been, but now would never be.

4

At last; farewell . . .

The next day was to be their last together and they celebrated it not, as one might expect, with a visit to the pub, but over breakfasts of miniature foodstuffs at the IKEA in Milton Keynes. Mma Ontoaste needed to do some proper shopping. They were sitting shoulder to shoulder in the cafeteria and wearing, with the exception of Carpaccia – who was trim in a navy-blue trouser suit with three wavy gold lines around the sleeve – slightly soiled Highland dress.

Tom was sunk in gloom and could hardly eat a thing. Mma Ontoaste forked the tiny egg from his plate and popped it in her own mouth. Carpaccia raised her beaker of orange-juice-style drink.

'Let's drink to all those we have left behind,' she suggested. They thought for a few seconds of Rambouillet, still lying slumped on the floor of the Richmond mansion; of Lemm Lemmingsson, just at that moment queuing at the video store on Hamngatan, waiting to take out a DVD of *Fanny and Alexander*; of Mma Pollosopresso, who was so badly treated and still unsure whether Mma Ontoaste blamed her for blowing up the tiny white van; and of Mary Shortbread, who never really came alive in any reader's imagination.

Tom raised his glass again.

'To us!' he said. 'Or rather, you!'

He gestured at the four detectives. A valedictorian atmosphere had settled on the quintet. The cafeteria was emptying now, shoppers getting ready to face the task of queuing to pay for their goods, and the four detectives were aware that they were in at the end of something. Their joint adventures had led them to this point and it was now over. Later they would be on their way, back to their own countries and their own particular problems. But this had been an adventure, an escape.

'Rra,' began Mma Ontoaste. 'I have enjoyed myself. It has been a road trip, class reunion and detective investigation all rolled into one.'

'But so many loose ends, Tom. Is there any way to sew them up? We could go through some now?'

Tom was staring into space. Eventually he spoke.

'No. There's no need. Let's just forget about them, shall we? After all, what do they really matter? What does anything really matter? It was fun. It is done. And now let's not try to read anything else into it.'

'That's a wee bit dark, Tom, what'll you call it?'

Tom waved a hand. What did he care?

'*Defective Detective*?'

'Hmm, nice. A wee bit modest for my taste, though. I'm toying with *Kernmantle*.'

'Kernmantle? What is Kernmantle?'

Sometimes it was good to have someone like Wikipedia around.

'It's a type of rope, but it mebbe sounds a wee bit Celtic, no?'

'What about McKernmantle?' Carpaccia suggested

'Aye, that's an idea.'

'Or you could put an exclamation mark on the end,' mumbled Colander. 'And emboss the front of your book.'

'Oh aye, what about you, then? What are you going to call yours, Mr Swedish Detective?'

'I am going to call mine *The Hour of the Wolf*. It sounds apocalyptic.'

'Apocalyptically boring is what I'm thinking. *The Hours and Hours and Hours of the Wolf*, more like. What about you, Faye?'

'I was going to call it *Unnatural Presumption*, to be a bit more like my other books, but now I think I'll use *The Music Man*. Zippier. And it taps into that whole nursery thing.'

There were nods of agreement.

'And what do you think you will entitle your book, Mma Ontoaste?'

'Oh, I don't know. *The Urine Trail of the Bull* or something like that.'

That made them sit back.

'That's kinda gross, Delicious, if you don't mind me saying so.'

'Well, Mma, it is easy and it sounds a bit sub-Saharan and so, why not?'

There was a brief discussion of deadlines. When they heard how fast Mma Ontoaste could write, the other three detectives drank their coffee.

'Well, I'll be away then,' said Rhombus.

He embraced Faye and then Mma Ontoaste and the tears welled in all their eyes. His brief handshake with Colander changed to a bear hug, with much pounding on the back. Meanwhile the girls were locked in a hug, promising to exchange gossip in the future. One by one they left the store – Colander and Ontoaste taking advantage of the taxi service to have themselves delivered to Heathrow to catch their planes, Rhombus to hitch north and Carpaccia to her submarine – leaving Tom alone. Alone in IKEA. Would that make a good title he wondered? *Alone in IKEA* by Tom Hurst.

No. It was rubbish. He knew he would never be a detective writer. He just didn't care enough and he could never get used to the fact that none of it was true and none of it mattered, or cast any light on anything, despite their claims of topicality.

He crushed the plastic cup in his hand and was about to stand up and follow when he saw a familiar figure. It was Alice Appleton.

'What are you doing here?' he asked.

'Looking for you,' she said. 'You have to come quick. Professor Wikipedia's been throttled.'

Who cared? It was bound to happen.

'Where's the Dean?' he asked.

'No one knows,' Alice replied.

There was a long silence. Tom saw the gleam of expectation in Alice Appleton's shining eyes.

'All right, then,' he said, collecting his pack of 50 Glimma tea lights, his jar of Lyngonsylt and the Smycka decoration stalks that his mother had asked him to get. 'Show me the body.'